D1429242

THE TRAIL DRIVERS

THE
TRAIL DRIVERS

by

JACK BORG

THE CHILDREN'S PRESS
LONDON AND GLASGOW

This Impression 1971

ISBN 0 00 165147 1

© THE CHILDREN'S PRESS

PRINTED AND MADE IN GREAT BRITAIN

CONTENTS

CONTENTS

CHAPTER ONE

DREAMS OF THE TRAIL

"WE NEED milk, Tim," said Mrs. Bryant. "Louise must have some, and there's none left in the crock. See what you can do, son."

"All right, Ma," Tim grinned at his baby sister, and waggled his fingers at her. Louise always thought this was cute, so he did it for her again before he went outside. "I'll get back as soon as I can," he told his mother. "Don't know how long I'll take."

Finding milk was a problem for the Bryant family. A city boy would just grab a jug and head for a dairy; but here, in the brush country, things were a little different. As a rule, nobody bothered much with milk; but, with a young baby around, an effort was made to get some when it was possible. The Bryants had owned a milch-cow, but it had eaten loco-weed a few weeks before and died; so now Tim had to rustle and locate milk wherever he could find it.

He was not sure how many cows his father owned. They ran over a lot of country and, as Mr. Bryant said, over anything else that got in their way! They were not dairy cattle but snuffy, ornery longhorns, with fire in their eyes and pure blazing brimstone in their tempers. Milking one of them was quite a chore.

He walked out into the sun, towards the horse-corral; tall for his fourteen years, dressed in clean but threadbare shirt and overalls. The overalls were nearly as brown as his skin, and had been patched pretty often. Nobody minded the patches. Where he lived, folks did not dress up except on Sundays and holidays.

Tonto came to meet him. Tonto was the hound pup which Ramon Chavez had given him; a kind of dusty lemon-coloured character, with one ear that floated higher than the other. At five months, Tonto was lanky and awkward, and hadn't filled out; most of the while there wasn't much to him, except a wag and a big grin.

Tonto's hind legs grew faster than the ones in front, so he had to hitch himself around corner-wise when he ran. If he forgot to do this, the legs sometimes tangled and tripped him up, but the fall made no difference to his boneheaded cheer-fulness.

Across at the corral, Tim lifted his rope from the post where he had left it, and roped out his pony. It was no trick to catch the horse, which was as old as Tonto was young, and only acted up a little, once in a while.

The pony's name was "Old Blue". He was a speckled roan with legs like stumps, all of them banged up with scars and swellings. His face looked as if he thought the world was a sinful place, but had quit trying to change it a long while ago.

Some of the cowhands made out that Blue had arrived on the American Continent with Columbus, although Tim did not think he was quite as aged as that. It was enough for Tim that Blue was a horse and could carry him around, so he didn't let the men's teasing worry him.

He saddled the old bronc, and waved to his mother and Louise after he climbed on board. They stood under the porch and waved back, until he turned around the edge of the clump of pecan trees that fringed the house and moved out of their sight.

Whistling, he heeled Blue along at an easy shuffle. Like most boys he had an urge to make a pony run, but knew it was no use trying that with Blue, who kept to his own pace whatever happened.

He was beginning to learn, too, that there was no sense in flogging a bronc along unless you had a good reason. If you did that, you might find yourself in a spot afterwards where you really needed some speed, only to find your horse was played out. And then, where were you? Besides, you could ruin a horse by running it too hard. And that wasn't just senseless; it was wicked.

For a while he rode on, looking about him. It

was still early. Although the sun was bright, the morning was cool; later, when the sun climbed, the day would be a blazer. But as yet the shadows were long and clean, and a pleasant breeze lifted Blue's mane.

The country through which he rode was partly grass and partly cactus brush, or *chaparral*, as it is often called. The brush grew in wild tangled thickets, of which some were many miles across. Often these were so dense that it was almost impossible to get through them, unless you knew the secret zigzag paths that wound through their depths. All sorts of hideous spiny growths flourished there; a hundred kinds of cactus, twining with mesquite, ebony, evergreen oak and countless others.

Between the clumps of *chaparral* lay grassy flats, which also varied greatly in size. The grass was short and curly, cured on the stem by the sunlight until it was like hay. Now and then Tim passed knots of grazing cattle. They glanced at him suspiciously with their great sweeping horns lifted, and trotted off into the brush if he came too close to them.

Tonto ran ahead of him and made a big fuss of sniffing around in the grass or the brush thickets. Unlike the longhorns, Tonto was long on good temper but short on brains. If he put up a bird or a jackrabbit, he lit after it like a crazy dog, but he never caught anything. If he found something which stood up to him, like a wild pig or a steer, he turned tail and ran instead, as he had no ambition to be a hero. Either way, it was all good, clean fun.

Tim jogged on steadily, keeping an eye open for a likely cow. First he had to find one with a calf, to be sure of getting milk; after that would come the livelier task of milking the cow.

He had travelled for about an hour when Tonto set up a racket of barking and raced ahead. Tim rounded a clump of mesquite to see another rider, who waited for him to come up. The rider sat a sorrel pony, almost as old as his own, and lounged in the saddle with a knee crooked over the horn.

"Hi," said Paul Barr. "Where you going?"

Paul was Tim's best friend; the youngest of the Barr family, who owned a place higher up Honey Creek. Paul was slim and skinny, as fair as Tim was dark, and a tuft of his pale, bleached hair stuck through a hole in his hat. His bright blue eyes held an impish glint, which told that he was not really as solemn as he looked.

Briefly Tim explained his errand, and Paul nodded. "I'll ride with you a ways," said Paul. "Can't stay too long, though. Right now, I'm supposed to be digging post-holes for that new pen Dad's building, and I'll sure know all about it if I don't get some done."

"All right," Tim nodded. He knew as well as Paul that his friend ought not to come with him, really. But, given the chance, he himself would rather chase cows than dig, any time. A fellow could spend all day, toiling and breaking his heart in the hot sun with a spade, and what did he have to show for it, at the end? Nothing but a little hole in the ground.

Then his conscience hit him. "If we get through this chore pretty soon, maybe I'll give you a hand," he said. "Don't think there'll be any more work for me to-day."

Paul moved his leg back to its proper position and shoved his boot into the stirrup. His smooth, tanned face did not change expression. After a pause he remarked: "Yesterday there was an ol' muley-cow of ours with a calf along, down in that blackjack *motte* by the creek swimming-hole. We could try for her, if you like."

"Thanks," said Tim. "She'd do fine. Let's go!"

Turning their ponies, they headed for the creek. On the way there they passed time by roping odd things which took their fancy, such as stumps and bushes; anything, in fact, which they could toss a loop over.

Paul made a show at roping Tonto, but the pup had been there before. Paul hardly swung the loop before Tonto was out of range, with a grin that said, "You don't catch me that way again, mister!—I know all the dodges now."

The boys never stopped using their ropes to practise fancy throws which they were learning.

At present, Tim was busy with a new *pial* which Ramon Chavez had shown him. Ramon was his father's *caporal*, or foreman, and was one of the finest ropers who ever touched a *reata*. As the cowhands said, he could "snake a mosquito out of a ball of tumbleweed!"

The throw took some doing, and Tim had not quite mastered it yet. You made the cast underhand, with a flick of the wrist which sent the loop in a quick twisting curve. The loop had to be the right size, and became a figure-of-eight during its flight. If it was too small, it wouldn't catch both hind legs of the cow, as it was meant to do; yet, if it was too big, it might hang up on a bough or something, and miss outright.

In that close, overgrown country, such a throw was very useful. This was not the open prairie, where only a good pony and a rope were needed. Here a man had to hunt his beef in stuff which grew so thick that many a prairie rider could not have hacked his way through it with a two-bitted axe.

Often the brush hand caught only a glimpse of his quarry as he slammed through the timber after it, and he had to be fast and accurate if he hoped to make a catch. So his throw had to be just right, with a small loop which did not miss.

Tim made a number of casts, and was pleased to see them come out pretty well. Not as slick as

Ramon would have made them, but fair enough for a start. Grudgingly, Paul said, "That isn't too bad. I'll take a shot at it myself. Show me how, again!"

Together, they made a few more tries as they rode along. "Your Dad was over to our place yesterday, talking to mine," said Tim, after a while. "Something about taking a herd up to Dodge. You hear anything about that?"

"Some," Paul admitted. "I was going to ask you if you had. Dad was talking to Layton about it. Seems like a bunch of the stockmen are going to gather beef, and they want your father to boss the drive."

Layton Barr was Paul's eldest brother, now in his early twenties. Probably Layton would go along, Tim thought, envying him. "I'd sure like to go," said Tim. "It would be grand, to ride up there with 'em. Say, that really would be something!"

Paul did not answer at once. Like Tim, he felt that it would be a wonderful adventure; every boy in Texas dreamed of riding up the trail, sooner or later. "Yes," he sighed at length, "it would be fine. They wouldn't take us, though. We're too young."

"Don't see why. They take boys sometimes, horse-wrangling and such. And we can ride herd as well as most grown cowhands, anyhow."

"Tim!" said Paul, with a catch in his voice.

"Tim, why don't you ask your Dad if he'll take us?"

"I'll ask him," Tim replied, with a sigh, "but don't count on it too strong. Dad isn't a man you can talk around; if he says a thing, he means it."

Truly he hadn't much hope, yet the notion stuck in his head. Maybe he could talk his Dad into it, although it would take some doing. And, anyhow, nobody could shoot a fellow just for asking.

Tim came out of his thoughts to find that they were moving down towards Honey Creek, with the sun dancing on the water and hitting white sparks from the ripples. The banks were overhung with vegetation in places, which cast trembling reflections that quivered in dark patches against the light.

At that moment, Paul exclaimed, "Hey, there's our ol' muley-cow yonder, in that patch of blackjack!"

Digging his heels into Blue, Tim sent the pony at a run towards the patch of *chaparral* on the creek bank. A glimpse of dun-coloured hide was visible through the brush, and a tail switched at flies lazily. Tim could not see the calf, but supposed it was around somewhere. It wouldn't stray far from its mamma.

CHAPTER TWO

The Dark Stranger

As Tim rode, he built a loop and let it dangle ready in his hand. Paul went wide of him, swinging his own rope in case it was wanted. By now they were right on the creek bank, close to the brush thicket which straggled down towards the water.

The dun-coloured body in the foliage went suddenly taut with suspicion, just as Tim sent his loop snaking through the branches at its heels. There was a loud snort, and a crashing in the undergrowth, and the cow burst into the open.

So far, everything was fine except for a few details. First was that Tim hadn't scored properly with his throw, which had caught only one leg instead of two. The second, and more interesting, was that he hadn't caught Barr's muley-cow, or even a cow at all. His victim was a mean, crusty *ladino* bull; a fierce outlaw, who very likely had never felt a rope before, and decided he didn't like it now!

The bull came slamming out of the brush with a scream like ten thousand brazen trumpets, and charged Tim with his head down and his tail high. Blue moved faster than he had ever done since Columbus's bosun herded him off the boat, skipped to one side as the bull foamed past.

Blue was a trained cowhorse, knew his job. Propping his forefeet, the ancient bronc squatted and braced himself to take the strain. Tim sat tight, hoping. His own end of the rope was tied to his saddle, and he waited for the terrific yank that was coming.

The next thing he knew was that he was pressing hard into the ground with his left ear. His hat was wedged down over his eyes, and he was scared rigid because he couldn't see. If the bull came for him, he was done!

Sprawled flat, he pushed the hat clear and saw Paul on the sorrel, cutting out a hot trail for the bull, which was chasing them. Whenever the sorrel dodged, the bull skidded to a halt and whipped around fast, lifting a cloud of dust. Tim's rope was still hitched to the bull's off hind leg, but the animal paid no heed to it; an object flapped and corkscrewed at the free end of the rope, raising more dust each time it bounced. It was Tim's saddle.

Tim knew what had happened. Like Blue, the saddle was long past its best. When a ton or so of hurtling beef hit the end of the *reata*, Blue and the rope did their duty, but the saddle quit. The jerk snapped the cinch which held it, and it went kiting away after the bull. Tim sailed with it.

Dizzily Tim scrambled to his feet. He was scratched here and there, and his ears were full of a ringing tone that made him feel like a human belfry, but he was not hurt. It struck him that it was time he got back into the act.

Paul's sorrel was tiring. Nearly as old as Blue, the poor brute wasn't able to keep up the pace much longer. If Paul and the horse did not get clear of the bull during the next minute or two, they were sure to be caught. The idea sent a cold ugly shudder up Tim's back. He had seen what an angry bull could do.

Blue stood nearby, made no move as Tim grabbed the dangling reins and skinned on to his bare back. Tim sent him up to the bit and was about to kick him into a run, but then paused for an instant in surprise.

At the edge of the patch of *chaparral*, three riders had appeared. They were strangers; Tim had never seen them before. Laughing, they watched Paul's antics as the boy dodged the bull.

The men sat the finest horses Tim had ever set eyes on, but were roughly dressed. They wore ordinary "brush-popper's" rig; frayed duck jumpers, leather chaps scarred with thorns, and battered hats with rawhide thongs knotted under their chins. All of them wore pistols.

The one in the middle lounged in his saddle, with an elbow resting carelessly on the swellfork. He was lean and swarthy, had a dark moustache and very white teeth, most of which showed when he laughed. The toothy whiteness reminded Tim of a dog grinning; but not a gentle harmless dog, like Tonto.

A blaze of hope warmed Tim, and he shouted, "Help me, please! We have to get that bull off Paul's tail!"

The dark man shifted his glance, and his sly grin widened. Tim got a shock when the bold black eyes met his own; they were strong and brilliant, held him for an instant as if they had the power to freeze him into helpless stillness, as a rattlesnake does with a bird. He shook off the feeling; but he was more scared than ever, just for that moment.

"What for?" asked the man, and the other two chuckled. "I'd say Paul was makin' out all right. Looks to me like he's havin' himself some fun!"

Tim could hardly believe his ears. He was no fool, and guessed that these were almost certainly some of the law's "wanted" characters, of whom there were many in Texas at that time. He knew, too, that Texas men were often hard and tough, even when they were honest; they had to be, to stand the life. But not many would stand by and watch folks in trouble, without lending a hand. What was wrong with these three?

He decided to waste no more time on them. With a queasy flutter just above his belt-buckle, he kicked Blue in the flanks and lined him out towards Paul and the bull. He didn't know what he could do, but he certainly aimed to do the best he could!

Blue had taken half a dozen strides, when a mutter of hoofs drummed behind him, growing swiftly louder as they overtook him. Tim's spirits lifted, and he could have snivelled with relief. The strangers had only joked with him after all, meaning to help all the while!

A wild cheer shrilled, and they passed him in a skimming rush like birds, yipping and giving sharp, piercing whistles between their teeth. They rode crazily, their bodies swaying in reckless ease. The dark man led, swerved in gracefully to crowd the bull from the side. The bull swapped ends instantly and charged him.

Tim did not see him draw the gun. The shot made a hard ringing crack, echoing down the creek in a chain of reports. For three more jumps the bull hurtled onward, then went down on his chin and slid two or three feet in a fume of dust. With a queer, faintly sick sensation, Tim realised that it was dead.

The man blew smoke from the muzzle of the six-gun as Tim arrived. He was still grinning as he said, "There you are, son. I guess that fixes your trouble." As he spoke, he opened the gate of the pistol's cylinder and thumbed in a new load, which he took from among the brass shells which studded his belt.

"Thanks," said Tim, who felt uncomfortable again under the power of that dark, mocking stare. "I—uh—we're a heap obliged."

"Don't you git to monkeyin' around with growed bulls another time. Anyhow, not until you've grown some, an' savvy what you're up against. They can be kind of tough!"

Tim believed him. He wanted to explain that he had thought the bull was a cow when he roped it, but figured that it would make him look even sillier if he did, so he kept his mouth shut. Awkwardly he slid off Blue's back as the two other men arrived and reined in by their leader, grinning at him.

"Figure he'll make a cowhand some day, Brazos?" asked one of them, a big, rangy fellow with rusty hair and a missing tooth. This man had high, hard-looking cheekbones and a long chin. His smirk made Tim furious, but he had enough sense not to show it.

"If he lives long enough," said Brazos. "He won't, if he tries to rope *ladino* bulls with an ol' crow-bait hoss an' rotten gear, though; because he'll git his fool self killed first."

The third rider was a Mexican; small and wiry, with an Indian cast in his coppery face. The Mexican said, "The boy have to learn. Nex' time he have more savvy, huh?"

Brazos replaced his six-shooter, his eye on Blue. "Say, what kind of a thing is that yuh're ridin'?"

he asked. "I didn't even figure it was livin', until I saw it crawl. Don't yuh have ponies, around these parts?"

"He's old," Tim admitted, "but he can get around. He's better than he looks."

"I sure hope so," said the rusty-haired rider. "If he wasn't, he'd have been dead an awful long time!"

Tim felt himself going red. This kind of talk wasn't any different from what he had to take from the cowhands he knew; friends and neighbours from local ranches. Yet, coming from these strangers, he didn't like it. Worse, he knew he was grateful to them really, because they had got Paul and himself out of a tight place, but he had to keep reminding himself of that, to keep from getting mad with them.

Paul arrived just then, nodded at the men dumbly. Paul's face was white under its sunburn, and the old sorrel was blowing hard, with its flanks pumping in and out. Dapples of foam creamed on its neck and flanks, and the hair of its hide was dark and soaking wet.

It struck Tim that Paul and the sorrel had taken a far tougher ride than he had himself. He knew Paul was scared. At that moment he understood that Paul must have gone right in and tolled the bull away from him, when he was on the ground. If Paul hadn't done that, the bull would have got him!

"Had a good ride, kid?" Brazos addressed Paul. Paul gulped, answered in a squeaky voice, "Pretty good, thanks. I was glad when you gentlemen showed up, though."

The men all laughed. "He has plenty of sand, anyhow," said the one whom Tim had already mentally christened "Rusty". "Guess they'll both make real cowhands, at that, long as they watch out what they drop their loops on."

"Sure," nodded Brazos. "If they do that, they'll be all right. Ain't likely to end up like us, then!"

Tim shot Paul a glance, knew his friend was thinking the same as he was himself; Brazos's joke meant only one thing, confirmed his original suspicion that these men were cow-thieves. Brazos was still grinning at him. "What's your handle, kid?" Brazos asked.

"Tim Bryant."

"Cal Bryant's boy?" The grin faded, replaced by a glitter of quick interest. "Is it true your ol' man's fixin' to trail a herd up to Dodge?"

"Why, I—uh——!" Tim hesitated, not liking to tell a stranger what little he knew of his father's plans.

"Don't lie, boy!" The grin was gone altogether and Brazos gave him a cold, chilly stare from which all the fun was gone. It still bore on him with that strange fascination, but now it was dangerous and menacing. "Is he?"

"He hasn't made up his mind, I guess," said Tim sullenly. He made himself fight against the threat in Brazos's manner. "Maybe he'd tell you, if you asked him."

The Mexican laughed softly. "Thees boy, he got plenty sand too," he said. " *¿ Que importe, amigos?* What does it matter? We will find out soon enough!"

Brazos relaxed, and his doggy smile returned. It was definitely ugly, this time. "That's right," he drawled. "It makes no odds. Come on, boys! We got to go places."

He whirled his fine bay gelding, and the three of them set off up the creek at a lope, taking no further notice of Tim and Paul.

When they had gone, Paul said, "They sure got us out of a hole, but I figure to be glad if we don't see 'em any more. Their company kind of gave me the hi-jimmy-diddlums!"

"Pretty good folks to keep away from, I'd say," growled Tim. He went to unhitch his rope from the dead bull's pastern. "All the same, I don't know what we'd have done if they hadn't shown up. We owe 'em that, at least!"

The saddle was banged up, but not much worse that it had been before, except for the broken cinch. That could be mended by sewing it together with rawhide. He slung it on Blue, and lashed it in place with his rope. "Now for that muley-cow," he grumbled. "We'll have to use your rope this time, *hombre*. And this time we'll catch the right one, by gosh!"

They found the muley-cow, so called because she had no horns, and her calf, soon afterwards. It was no trick to drive the animals back to the Bryant home. The fun began when they tried to get them into the corral. The old cow would not go past the gate, until Tim roped the calf and made it follow him inside. The cow followed then, and began a performance almost as lively as the one the bull had given.

However, the boys got out and left her in there with the calf, knowing it was useless to begin the circus of trying to milk her until she had settled down. Later, when she accepted the fact that she was not going to be hurt, she might be persuaded to yield a drop of milk. Tim hoped!

They went across to the house, and told Mrs. Bryant what they had done, but did not mention their adventure with the bull.

"That's fine," said Mrs. Bryant. "Your Dad's making a dicker with Mrs. Fennell for one of her milk-cows. If she will sell, you won't have to go through this business any more, son."

"Good," said Tim. "It sure is a pesky job, trying to squeeze a drop of juice from one of those babies."

"Dooce," said Louise. "Babies. Dooce-babies!"

"That's it," said Paul. "Juice for babies. Cow-juice."

"Cow-dooce," Louise repeated. She went on

saying it whilst Tim hesitated. After a moment Tim asked his mother, "Say, Ma . . . Uh! . . Do you—do you think Dad would take Paul and me with him, up the trail?"

Mrs. Bryant looked at him, her face going serious all at once. She turned her back, and said in a queer, dry tone, "I don't know, Tim. You'd better ask him."

Outside, Paul snickered. "That was the answer you gave that Brazos fellow, remember?" he said. "Looks like your Dad will have to answer quite a few questions."

Tim had borrowed another saddle from one of the *vaqueros*. He threw it on Blue, answered, "Come on. We have a few post-holes to dig, or you'll be answering some questions. And your Dad will be asking 'em!"

"He sure will," Paul agreed, mounting the sorrel. "We'd better hustle and fix him with the right answers too, or else!"

Together they rode out of the yard and headed for the place where Mr. Barr was going to build his new corral. Both of them were trying not to hope too much. But it would be grand, to ride up the trail to Dodge!

CHAPTER THREE

BRUSH-POPPERS

CAL BRYANT said, "Tim, you and Paul stay there with Vicente." He pulled his mouse-coloured bronc around, added, "Watch those critters real close. They'll hit back for the brush, if they see half a chance."

Tim nodded. "All right, Dad." They were on a grassy flat outside a big mesquite thicket, which was known to harbour a lot of steers. Already a number had been chased out of there and gathered into a herd, which the boys had been set to hold whilst riders combed the brush for more.

Mr. Bryant ran his eye over the uneasy cattle, then grinned at the boys. "You'll have plenty of exercise, herding that bunch of gunpowder," he said. And then, jokingly, "You let one of them run, and I'll surely make you hard to catch, yourselves. That's a promise!"

"Don't worry," Tim grinned back. "Won't be any of them get clear, Dad. We'll hold 'em slick as dairy cows!"

In his own mind, Tim was sure that no steer was going to get away from him. This was one time he and Paul had to show they could work as well as anybody, and they meant to prove it.

With a chuckle and a wave of the hand, his father legged the pony back into the mesquite. Tim heard him thrusting deeper into the brush, making a rattle and scrape of leather against boughs, and knew there would be something doing pretty soon.

He caught Paul's eye, across the bunched steers, and laughed. Paul smiled back at him. Both boys were highly delighted, felt important and, for the present at least, in a nobly dutiful frame of mind. They were going north, to Dodge!

Remembering, Tim felt again the lump in his chest, that rose to hamper his breath when he braced his father. When it came to the point, he had trouble getting the words out, but swallowed and then made himself speak his piece.

"Take you with me?" Mr. Bryant repeated, frowning, when Tim got through. Tim thought it was finished; he was going to be turned down. But all his father said was, "I don't know about that. I'll have to talk to your Ma."

"I asked her, Dad," Tim exclaimed pleadingly. His tone quickened with anxiety. "She said to ask you!"

Cal Bryant rubbed his straw-coloured moustache with one finger, which was a habit he had when he was thinking. "All right," he grunted, after a moment. "I'll bear it in mind."

Tim was on hooks, could hardly bear the strain of waiting until he knew for certain. He heard his parents talking after he had gone to bed, and wondered if they were discussing him. Maybe his mother wouldn't want him to go, he thought. Like all mothers, she was scared in case something awful happened to him when she wasn't around to handle it, and wished he'd stay at home where she could see him.

To his joy, next day his father said, "Well, I had it out with your Ma. I have to admit she doesn't go for the idea, but she understands you'll have to grow up some time. She's willing for you to go."

Tim couldn't say anything at first. He was too full of sixty different feelings to be able to speak.

"But, mind!" his father went on. "From now on, you're a man, and you'll work like one. You're taking on a mighty tough chore, and you won't be able to quit if you find that you don't like it . . . Don't forget that!"

Tim could have walked on the ceiling. He gave a whoop that would have scared a Comanche and ran indoors to hug his mother, then tossed Louise in his arms until she crowed with delight, as happy as himself. Next thing, he was on Old Blue and heading for the Barr place to tell Paul, as fast as Blue could lick.

Paul's father, Gabriel Barr, looked down his nose at first when he heard. "Your Dad's taking you?" Mr. Barr grumbled. "Don't see why Paul has to go too, just because of that. I was figuring on keeping him here, with me. Layton and Ollie are going, and that'll leave us short-handed."

Paul's face fell, but he knew better than to whine. The Barrs did not encourage snivellers. Looking at him, Mr. Barr growled, "Oh, well. I guess I'll never hear the last of it if Tim goes and you get left behind." His leathery face was red, like old brick, and seemed to crinkle around the eyes when he smiled. "Maybe you'll wish you stayed home before you're there, son. . . ! You don't need to act like crazy, yet. Your Ma will have something to say about it, first!"

Mrs. Barr said plenty, but the boys talked her into it after a while. It wasn't easy, but they got her round. She made Tim promise to see that Paul didn't sleep in damp blankets and remembered to change his socks, and a few dozen other things.

Tim promised, keeping his face straight while Paul went red and squirmed. Neither he nor Paul were worried about damp blankets, just then. At that time, they didn't know what they were to face later on.

Next day Mr. Bryant and his neighbours began to make the big gather, the task of hunting beef out of the *chaparral* in readiness for the drive. It was planned to send fifteen or sixteen hundred head, all of which had to be caught and branded.

They took some rounding up, in the trappy, over-grown brush, where they lived.

The boys kept the cattle bunched, outside the thicket. As Tim's father had forecast, they had plenty of fun holding them. With Vicente Chavez, the son of the Bryants' foreman, they were kept busy all the while. The steers were wild and nervous; a good many had never had any contact with man before, and they were as untamed as hawks. Every now and then one would make a break for the timber, and Tim or one of the other boys had to turn him back.

Vicente was a good hand with cattle. Like most Mexican riders, he was amazingly skilful with a horse or a rope, and seemed to know what the cows were going to do before the beasts knew it themselves. He laughed a lot, and sang to the cows a good deal of the time.

Presently Tim heard what he was waiting for. A high yell lifted, away in the brush, and was answered by others. In a few minutes there were other sounds. A crashing, tearing racket, made by heavy bodies careering through close under-growth. Next instant half a dozen big rangy steers came barrelling out into the open, with Mr. Bryant and Layton Barr after them.

The new steers joined the herd, and the riders went back into the brush to hunt for more. The life of a brush-hand holds more risks than that of any other cowboy; most of the time he is working deep in dense, thorny timber, tearing a hole through the branches however thick and tough they may be.

At full speed, when he chases a steer, he hangs on to his pony as best he can, crouched low and dodging the boughs which rip and tear at him. Cactus thorns and stubs of limbs snag his clothing and scratch his flesh, yet every instant he is ready with his rope, eager to throw his small loop the first chance he gets. Reckless and often bleeding, on his hurtling, jumping, swerving horse, he slams through the brush with an arm up to protect his face from the jabbing spiny limbs.

The Bryants, the Barrs, the Chavez men were all of this kind; true "brush-poppers" who could go booming at top speed through the worst thickets, and rope out the toughest outlaw steers and make them behave.

During the day, the bunch of animals which the boys herded grew until, late in the afternoon, the riders came from the brush and joined them. Now it was time to drive the steers to the pen, which the Barrs had just built. The pen was several miles distant, and Mr. Bryant and the other men wanted to get there with the steers before dark. Otherwise, they were likely to lose most of the beasts they had rounded up, and their day's work would be wasted.

They had more fun driving the steers. The creatures took off like a cavalry charge to begin with, and had to be slowed down by horsemen racing to head them. But, after a while, they lined out more quietly and allowed themselves to be driven.

Dusk was close when they reached the pen. As soon as the cattle saw the pen they began to act up again, milled and fought to break away. More time was spent, holding them and crowding them inside. At length the last bellowing longhorn was hazed through the gate, which was closed thankfully and barred.

By then it was full dark. A fire was going, throwing ruddy flickers over the grass and bushes. The tired dusty riders stripped and hobbled their ponies, turned them loose to graze, and came to the fire with their saddles and gear, to drop and rest.

"Phew! I'm plenty glad that chore's over," said Gabriel Barr, mopping his face with his faded yellow bandanna scarf. "Anybody who figures he needs exercise, just let him try chousing a bunch of *bronco* steers out of this brush, around here! I guarantee he'll get all the work-out he wants."

Cal Bryant, Tim's father, squatted on his heels by the fire, holding a tin cup of boiling coffee and swapping it from one hand to the other, because it was too hot to hold for long. "They'll be about enough," said Mr. Bryant. "We can start the drive any time."

"How many d'you count we gathered?"

Mr. Bryant looked across at the pen, where a forest of horns tossed against the starry sky and the lost, mournful bawling of the cattle had begun to die down. "Around fifteen hundred head," he replied, and took a sip at the coffee. "Fifteen hundred and eight, I made it. Could be there's one or two old scalawags that will have to be cut out, not worth even the price of their hides. But only a few."

"We brand to-morrow?"

Cal Bryant nodded. "Begin as soon as there's enough light, and get it done with as quick as we can. I want to start driving; the earlier we hit Dodge, the better the market."

Tim and Paul were cooking and tending the fire, listened to the men talking. They were eager to hit the trail, too. To them it loomed as an incredible adventure, full of tremendous possibilities; in Texas, at that time, it meant something to be able to say that you had been "up the trail."

These big cattle-drives were of fairly recent origin. In the years which had gone by since the end of the Civil War, times had been hard for Texans. Having been on the losing side in the war, they were ruined, with the rest of the South. There was no money, anywhere.

Then, to pierce the gloom of poverty and defeat, a ray of hope came. Cattle grazed on the Texas ranges, half wild and uncounted; millions of them—cattle, for which there was no available market and which were almost worthless, until a few courageous stockmen decided to drive their herds north and take a chance on selling them there.

Some of the early drives were disastrous, losing cattle, money and men; but others succeeded. Soon, vast numbers of steers trailed up to Kansas every summer, to reach the new markets which the recently-built railroads had brought into being. The money from the beef helped Texas to struggle to her feet again.

Hearing his father and the others talk, Tim Bryant was alert for every word as he went about his chores around the fire. What was it really like, he wondered? Were the tales true, the yarns of fights with Indians and cattle-thieves, of stampedes and Jayhawkers?

In time, he was to find out.

CHAPTER FOUR

RETURN OF BRAZOS

"GIT THAT fire going, boy," grumbled Frenchy. "Land sakes, you aim to set there an' hatch it?"

Frenchy Debrelle was a skinny, leather-hided old man with a stiff leg and a pair of grey whiskers that branched out in large curves, making him look a bit like a longhorn himself. He limped around to the back of the wagon and let down the tailboard, began to slam and bang his pots and pans around irritably.

Tim could have given him an answer, but kept his mouth shut. He knew Frenchy would be in a better temper soon, when the fire was hot enough, and the old boy could get on with his cooking. Trail cooks were notoriously grouchy.

"All right," Tim soothed. "Won't be but a few minutes."

"Huh! Better not be. Pretty soon you're goin' to see a bunch of hard, hungry *hombres* ride in here, and if there ain't anything for 'em to eat, they're liable to start in and eat yuh!"

Tim laid down a handful of dry grass, and covered it with a few twigs which he took from the rawhide "'possum-belly" which hung under the chuck-wagon. Firewood was scarce along the trail, and was used with care. He lit the grass and then, when the twigs caught, fed the blaze delicately with dry cowchips. If wood was rare, cowchips were plentiful and made a good substitute. In a little while he had a respectable fire going.

After he had helped Frenchy with other tasks, he went out to the horse-herd. Paul was already with the ponies. In general, it was the boys' work to look after the saddle-stock, although they had plenty of other chores to handle as well.

Often one or the other of them was required to join the beef herd, riding behind in the drag, whilst the other went on with Frenchy and the chuck-wagon, driving the loose horses at the same time. To-day, both had travelled with the *remuda*, as the bunch of spare horses was called, and were expected to help the cook in addition to tending the ponies.

"You'd better skin back and grab yourself a bite," said Tim, when he reached Paul. "If you wait until the rest of the outfit shows up, you won't have much time for eating."

"All right," Paul turned his pony. "Say, you didn't figure this out just to land me with a flock of greasy plates to clean after supper, did you?"

"Me?" Tim sounded injured. "What makes you think I'd do a thing like that?"

"Nothing. Only you did it yesterday, and the day before."

Tim sighed, wagged his head sadly. "I honestly don't know what's going to become of you, sonny," he said in a pitying tone. "I promised your Ma I'd look out for you, but as soon as I fix you with a nice, clean, safe, little job, you start right in to beef about it. For Pete's sake, what do you want?"

"I want you to handle the wash-up, Gran'pa, for a change! I'll take first shift at night-hawk, too, if you don't mind. Seems to me you've been making too many easy scores, lately!"

"Maybe you'd like Frenchy to rig you a bed in the wagon, too, so you can ride easy instead of polishing your pants on a saddle?" Tim sneered. To listen to them, one would think they were always quarrelling, but this was only their idea of fun. Each knew the other could be relied on in a pinch, and the insults they exchanged were meant to be friendly.

"I would," Paul admitted, "but I doubt if he'd do it. I don't aim to ask him, anyhow."

Tim grinned. "O.K. Ride it to the wagon and grab a bite, then come back. There'll be time, if you treat Frenchy right."

"Fine," said Paul, turning his pony. "See you later, Gran'pappy!"

Tim watched him hit a lope towards the camp, then put the ponies to graze and got the night horses ready. The night-herds used horses chosen especially for the work, and would expect to find these handy as soon as they had eaten their supper. That finished, Tim had nothing to do but wait for Paul to return and take over the first shift at night-herding the horses.

Yawning, he pushed his hat back off his forehead and looked back along the way they had come. The country up here was open, rolling away in waves of empty grassland, unlike the brush-grown *chaparral* he had known at home. A smear of dust lifted into the sky and betrayed the approach of the beef herd. It would be here pretty soon, he decided.

Not for the first time, he told himself that there was nothing much to trail-driving, after all. Nothing, that was, except a lot of work and hardly any sleep. It had taken them nearly a month to reach this spot, and still they had three hundred miles to go. He wondered what had become of the marvellous adventures that were to have made life dangerous and exciting; up to now, during those weary weeks of travel, nothing remarkable had happened at all.

Every day at dawn, the same old routine began again. Frenchy packed up his chuck-wagon and drove ahead to find a suitable camp for the next night, and the cattle were headed north, moving about twelve miles a day. The crew walked them on gently, let them scatter at midday to graze awhile, and then drove again until late afternoon.

Tim did not see much of his father. As trail boss, Mr. Bryant was a busy man. Much of the time he scouted far in front of the herd. It was his task to find the best route, where the grazing was good; to watch for dangers to be avoided, and a dozen other things. Only at night, when he came into camp, did he and Tim find a chance to talk.

The beef herd was close now. Tim watched it, snaking in a long, long line out of the distance, the drag still hidden in the pall of dust stirred up by the plodding hoofs. Paul's brother, Ollie Barr, and a man named Will Dunford were at point, ahead of the lead steers, and the swing riders kept the beasts in line along the flanks.

When Tim or Paul worked with the herd, they had to ride in the drag, the place where young or inexperienced hands were always put, pushing the laggards along. It was no pleasant job, choking in the thick of the dust lifted by the herd in front, but the boys did not mind. They were going up the trail, and would have stood a good deal worse, and liked it, for the sake of the distinction it gave them.

He came out of his thoughts, to see Paul racing back to him from the chuck-wagon. Paul was in a hurry, pushed his bronc along. Old Blue and the sorrel had been left at home; nowadays both boys used a string of horses from the *remuda*, like the other hands.

"What's wrong?" asked Tim, as Paul reined the pony to a skidding halt. "Prairie afire, or something?"

Then he saw Paul's face, and the look on it stopped him from making any more jeering remarks. Paul was anxious and tight-lipped, plainly upset. Disregarding Tim's question, he replied, "Say, you know those three fellows we met, the day we roped that bull?"

A slight flutter made itself felt under Tim's ribs. "What about 'em?" he replied, in a voice which he tried to make careless, but which sounded strained, even to himself.

"They're in camp," said Paul. "Talking to Frenchy, and wolfing his grub."

"Did they say anything to you?"

"They let on they'd never seen me before," said Paul, "but made kind of funny cracks, to show they were on to me. They knew me, all right."

"What do they want?"

Paul shrugged. "*¿Quien sabe?*" he said.

Like most Texans, the boys spoke Spanish as well as they spoke their own tongue. When Paul asked, "*Who knows?*", Tim wished there was some way of finding out. The news that Brazos and his two partners had shown up gave him an edgy feeling of discomfort.

"You figure they're up to something?" Paul asked him quickly.

"Dunno," Tim was doubtful. "Why should they be?"

"They acted plenty queer, not saying right out that they knew me, and that Brazos *hombre* was grinning at me like a coyote. I didn't like it one bit!"

Tim felt uneasy as he rode back to camp for his own meal. Why had those three mavericks shown up here, so far from the place where they had last met? It might be an accident, but he had an awkward notion that it wasn't.

It was true that they had got Paul and himself out of a tight place; yet, in spite of that, he did not trust them. They were outlaws, he was sure, and probably cow-thieves. He remembered that Brazos had asked him about the trail-herd, when it was not even certain that the drive was going to be made, and that bothered him more than ever. He did not know why he suspected them, but he could not rid himself of the feeling that they meant trouble.

By now the herd had arrived, and the hands were settling it on its bed-ground. Gradually the steers lay down, or began to graze, and some of the riders left them, to head for the chuck-wagon. The hands beat Tim into camp, and were already eating when he got there.

Brazos and the other two strangers squatted by

the fire, talking with the crew. Brazos was laughing, his white teeth bared in his thin, brilliant smile, and some of the trail hands laughed with him. Rusty and the Mexican kept silent, looking around them with idle curiosity whilst they ate hungrily.

Perhaps they had only dropped in for a meal, in the way cow-country folks did, thought Tim. Nobody ever thought of denying hospitality to a stranger, which would have been the worst of bad manners. He tried to convince himself of this, as he got his supper.

Vicente Chavez was filling his plate at the same time. A dark-skinned youngster, Vicente was about a year older than Tim; they had been reared together from baby days. Normally Vicente was cheerful and full of songs, but now he looked solemn, even faintly scared. If Tim had been less concerned with his own troubles, he would have asked Vicente what was wrong, but now he barely noticed the Mexican boy's expression.

With his plate in his hand, Tim sneaked behind the wagon in the hope that Brazos's crowd had not noticed him. He found he had little appetite, although he had been famishing not ten minutes before. He was almost forcing the meal down, when a shadow fell across his plate.

He knew who it was, even before he glanced up. Brazos stood there, lounging and sneering down at him with his toothy dog's grin.

"Howdy," said Brazos. "Yuh here, too?" As if it were a secret joke between the two of them, the outlaw chuckled softly.

Tim did not say anything. In spite of his loss of appetite, he wanted to go on eating, if only to show that he wasn't impressed by Brazos; but, somehow, he could not do it. Once again he sensed the power in the dark bright eyes, the hold which they exerted on him. He could only stare back.

"Me and my pardners are strangers around here," said Brazos. "We'd admire to have it stay that way. Savvy?" As if by accident, his hand rested gently on the butt of the big pistol which was anchored to his leg by a rawhide thong.

The flutter under Tim's ribs suddenly became an acute pang, which darted right through him. Dumbly he gazed at the outlaw, who towered over him as he squatted with his forgotten tin plate on his knee. After a space he gulped and croaked, "I savvy."

"That's dandy. Better tell your friend too, uh? We don't want an unlucky chance to happen to somebody, if we have to come back to find yuh. Do we?"

Tim managed to say that a chance like that was the last thing he wanted to happen, and Brazos chuckled again. "I can see yuh're a smart boy," said Brazos. "Just see yuh don't forget what I told yuh, that's all." With that, he nodded and went back to his friends.

Looking after him and seeing his easy, confident swagger, Tim felt anger stir beneath his fright. Who did Brazos think he was, he asked himself? It was reasonable to expect that men of his kind liked plenty of privacy, and no gossip when they travelled, but there was no need to get so tough about it.

On the heels of this, another angle occurred to him. Neither he nor Paul knew who Brazos really was, or either of his running-mates either, for that matter. Why should Brazos act so ugly then, out here where there was no law to bother them? Were they really planning mischief, as Paul suggested?

Brooding, he watched them thank Frenchy for the meal. The old man was offhand and surly with them, as he was to nearly everybody, but it seemed to Tim that he was less outspoken about it than he would have been to most folks. The three got their broncs and swung up into their hulls, then hit north with a wave of their hands. The last Tim saw of them was their figures, silhouetted almost black against the evening sky, as they topped a rise in the prairie and vanished.

He was miserable, turning the incident over in his mind whilst he washed the dishes and acted as flunkey for the cook. Neither he nor Paul had mentioned their adventure with the bull, mainly because they didn't want to be made fun of by their friends, or scolded by their parents for playing the fool.

Now he wished his father would come back. He wanted badly to tell all about it, because he could not get rid of a notion that Brazos and trouble were two different ways of saying the same thing, and he was scared of what lay in the future. Then he remembered that big six-gun, and the way Brazos handled it, and was more scared still.

When his father returned to camp, Tim avoided him. He heard his father say to Layton Barr and the others, "We hit the Red River to-morrow, boys. She isn't too high, so we should make a good crossing."

"What's the current like, Cal?"

"Fast, but not too deep. With luck, we'll be over without any trouble, this time to-morrow."

Without trouble, thought Tim? How he hoped that was true!

CHAPTER FIVE

RED RIVER VALLEY

THEY CROSSED the Red River next day. It rolled, fast and yellow in a rapid, sliding current but, as Cal Bryant had said, was not too deep. Frenchy Debrelle went first, with the chuck-wagon. Frenchy drove the team at an angle into the water heading upstream, and the wagon rocked crazily as it sailed across the deepest part of the river bed. Finally it struck solid ground again, and the old man drove his ponies up the bank, cracking his whip and bawling at them like a lunatic.

The *remuda* was to go next, to give the cattle a lead. Cal Bryant scowled at the boys, fingering his blond moustache. The crossing was not very dangerous, but Tim knew he was anxious. Mr. Bryant said, "Figure you can make it?"

"Sure. We'll do it easy," Tim answered. "There's nothing to it, Dad."

Tim tried to make his voice sound as if taking forty broncs across a river was a job he did every day. He and Paul were both good swimmers; besides, he guessed that his father had plenty on his mind, without having to fuss about their safety.

The job of a trail boss was to see that his beef got to market in good shape, and sell it. Above all, this herd had to make a profit. Like many Texans at that time, Mr. Bryant and his neighbours were poor, had nothing but their cattle; and the other stockmen, back home, were depending on the money from the sale of the beasts. The boys knew that the real reason why they had been allowed to come was that it saved wages. There was not enough money to hire paid hands.

"All right," said Cal Bryant. "Head upstream like Frenchy did, and try to make the place where he landed. Think you can do that?"

Tim nodded. "We'll do it or bust," he said.

"That's the spirit, son! Don't take any fool chances, and sing out if you hit trouble. Are you all set?"

The whole crew had stripped to their underwear, most of which was of the longhandled red flannel variety, and carried their clothes and boots to keep them as dry as possible. They looked a comic bunch, riding around like that, with their hats on.

Although the day was warm, Tim shivered as he inched his pony down the bank. He was riding a chunky, short-barrelled dun called Biscuit which he had chosen for its strength and pluck. Drumming his naked heels into Biscuit's flanks, he sent the pony into the current.

He looked across at the spot where Frenchy had

pulled out, on the other side, and tried to forget the river. A glimpse of creamy-brown, curling eddies, and whorls of foam, made him try harder still. He was afraid that, if he looked at them too long, his nerve might suffer. A high, shrill whoop pealed out behind him. He yelled in echo, and forced the bronc headlong into the racing water.

The river was cold, and up to his thighs as they plunged. It had a strong sly pull, tugging sidelong to draw him and Biscuit downstream, but the pony fought against it stubbornly. Above the muttering hum of the water, he heard the other horses splashing in after him. There was plenty of yelling and whistling. He snatched a glance behind him. Paul and Vicente Chavez were just following the tail of the *remuda* down the bank.

After that he had to concentrate on getting across. Biscuit was already swimming. The pony forged across the current, bucking it with all the strength he had; Tim felt the power of the horse, alive and surging under him, and was glad of it. It gave him a glorious feeling of elation.

The shelving bank, where Frenchy had landed, took an endless time to reach. At one moment, Tim was afraid he was going to miss it and drift too far down, where the bank was steep and there was no way of getting out. Desperately he turned Biscuit higher upstream.

He was wondering whether Paul and Vicente

would manage to drive the other horses after him, when Biscuit plunged, half drowning him in a bath of spray. Tim hung on tight. For some reason, the thing which bothered him most was that his bundled clothes were now wet, after all the trouble he had taken to hold them high out of the water.

Biscuit came up blowing and snorting, shook his mane violently and then crabbed downstream, swimming strongly. Almost at once he plunged again, and Tim felt his hoofs scrape the bottom. With a lurch and a scramble, Biscuit gained a footing, then plunged through the last shallow yards, straight for the landing place. They were across!

He turned, to see the *remuda* coming out after him. Paul and Vicente were still in midstream, urging them on. Vicente clung to his saddle-horn, looked green and scared, but did his job gamely enough. Only then did Tim recall that the Mexican youth could not swim. He yelled to encourage him, waving and grinning, and Vicente grinned back with a spark of his old high spirits.

Already the beef herd had begun the crossing. Tim's father came first, with a big brindle steer named Davy. Davy had taken his place as the leader of the herd on the first day, and had kept it ever since. Every man in the crew understood that where Davy went, the rest would follow, and Mr. Bryant kept close to him to see that he made the crossing without trouble. If Davy got over, the herd would come too.

Riders entered the water on each side of the long line of steers, most of them on the downstream flank. All the while they were urging, uttering hard, flat cries and whistling between their teeth, to keep the animals moving. The herd looked like a snake; a crawling, floating monster as it threaded from bank to bank. The beasts swam with their heads pushed forward and their chins on the surface, so that the water seemed to bristle with horns.

A yell from Frenchy caught Tim's attention. The cook had unhitched and already had a fire alight. Goodness only knew how he had done it in the time. Now he was calling for Paul to come and help him get a meal ready. He wanted chips collected for fuel, water drawn and other chores done; the hands would be tired and beaten, famished with hunger after they had got through the chore of driving the herd across.

Tim and Vicente hobbled the *remuda*, held it near the bank a short distance above the ford. Every now and then, men would be coming to change horses, leave their used-up broncs to rest, and mount fresh ones. The boys themselves would also have work to do shortly, giving help with the herd.

But, for the moment, they watched the steers coming across. Tim gauged how far his father still had to swim with Davy. Cal Bryant rode his bronc right against the steer, nudging Davy upstream when he showed a tendency to drift. Tim's gaze shifted to the landing place. It was then that he saw the tracks of the other horses.

All his excitement and interest in the crossing faded, like a lamp going out. There were three sets of tracks, none of them made by their own ponies. But Tim would have known that, anyhow. He had seen the prints before, last night at the chuck-wagon.

Brazos and the two others were ahead. The knowledge gave him a queasy shiver again for a moment, reminded him of how he had felt when Brazos spoke to him. He tried to shrug off the sensation, telling himself that the outlaws just chanced to be going in the same direction as themselves. There was no need for him to begin giving himself nightmares in broad daylight. Very likely Brazos was miles in front, by now.

He turned to say something to Vicente. The Mexican boy had also seen the tracks, and was now gazing down at them with the same look of fright he had shown when he crossed the river.

Tim braced him, "What's wrong, Vicente?"

Vicente started and jerked a quick glance up at Tim, his dark eyes wide and alarmed. Tim remembered that he had looked scared last night, at supper. It came to him then that it was not the swimming which had frightened Vicente; the

Mexican boy had something else on his mind.
Vicente was already afraid, before he pushed out
into the waters of the Red River. Tim wondered
whether they were both scared by the same
person.

"What is it?" Tim insisted. "Do you know
those men?"

Vicente gulped with an effort, and nodded
guiltily. In Spanish he replied, "I know the
Mexican. He is a distant cousin of my mother."

"How about Brazos? You know him too?"

"No, *amigo*," Vicente shook his head vigorously.
"I don't want to know him, either. He is bad
medicine! *Plenty* bad!"

"Who is he?"

"Brazos? He is Brazos Lamb. You mean you
did not know that?"

Stunned, Tim gaped at Vicente. Everybody had
heard of Brazos Lamb, sometimes called "The
Black Sheep". The old, awful thrill of cold ran
up through his belly as he sat there on Biscuit,
dumb and paralysed. Whatever had he got himself into?

Lots of men were called Brazos, simply because
they came from around the Brazos country. That
was why he hadn't paid any great attention to the
nickname. It was common enough, meant little
to him when he first heard it. But there was only
one Brazos Lamb!

There were plenty of tales about Lamb, and

Tim had heard most of them. Brazos had been a soldier in the Confederate Army, and had a good war record. After the War he came home to nothing. He was penniless and hard put to it to find a living, like many another.

Until then he was honest, and well thought of by his friends. Even when he quarrelled with a Northern agent, appointed by the occupying Federal troops, and shot him, most Texans were willing to help him escape from the military. Too many Northern officials were dishonest and greedy, tyrannising over the defeated South and robbing the people of anything they could. It was felt that Brazos was not greatly to blame for such an incident.

Afterwards Brazos "went on the dodge", outlawed by the Federals. It was then that his reputation began to suffer amongst Texans. Brazos drifted into outright criminality, became well known for his exploits as a robber and for his general bad character. Soon no one, except men of his own breed, wanted to be his friend. Cattle-thief, bandit, gunfighter, he was an enemy to all honest people.

It took nearly all day to get the herd across. The trail hands drove the lead steers on to a flat meadow near camp, and halted them whilst the rest came across. Tim and Vicente had to help ride herd on the beasts, holding them and setting them to graze, as more and more were driven up from the river. They were too busy, during that time, to think of Brazos Lamb.

Only in camp, after supper, did matters come to a head. Tim was saddling his pony, ready to go out on night herd, when a voice called his name. He turned, and saw his father looking at him.

"I've been watching you, son," Cal Bryant said. His face was grave, questioning. "Looks like you have some trouble on your mind. What's worrying you, boy?"

Tim felt his throat seize up. No words would come. His instinct was to blurt out that nothing was the matter, but he could not; he and his father had always been open with each other, and they never held secrets.

They were alone, else even then Tim might not have been able to tell. It came out, in a blundering rush of words. "That fellow was Brazos Lamb," he blurted.

"Which fellow?"

Tim told the whole tale, and Cal Bryant listened without interrupting. When Tim had finished, Mr. Bryant said softly, "Brazos Lamb? Well, we'll watch out, just in case; but I figure there are enough of us to finish anything he might start. Don't worry, Tim. He won't hurt us. And I'm glad you told me!"

CHAPTER SIX

TERROR IN THE NIGHT

THEY LEFT the banks of the Red, and pushed on into the Indian Territory. This is now the State of Oklahoma, but in those days it was set apart for the Indian tribes by government treaty. A number of white men lived there also. Most of these were either government agency employees or law-dodgers. Not many of them worked for the agencies.

At first they met with low sandstone hills, threaded by grassy valleys and brush-grown draws. Most of the brush was jackpine, dwarf-oak and hickory, with little of the prickly *chaparral* which the boys had known at home.

The weather changed, too. As they moved north, the clear sunny skies which had covered them nearly all the way up through Texas were replaced by sullen ones. By the time they reached open plain country again, dull, purplish clouds hung over the Wichita hills far to the northwest, piling high and lanced through with capering flickers of lightning.

The wind blew sultry and warm, only to change with fitful suddenness to bitter cold, and then back again. Nights grew colder, also. Just before dawn the chill waked them, shivering in their blankets.

Plodding, they walked the cattle on. The tracks of Brazos and the others vanished soon after they left the Red River, and had not been picked up since, although Cal Bryant and the older Barr brothers scouted on both sides of the route.

Their methods of trailing had been altered, too. Instead of ranging in front with the horses, as before, Tim and Paul travelled with the herd, keeping the *remuda* out on the flank. Even Frenchy kept fairly close. Cal Bryant did not expect trouble, but was taking no chances.

"Just as well to be prepared," he said. "Likely those fellows never aimed to bother us, but we'll be good and ready for them if they do."

The men carried rifles slung under their thighs, in addition to the six-guns which nearly everybody wore on a journey, in those days. The sight heartened Tim. "At least," he thought, "Brazos won't have things all his own way, if he tries to get smart."

Aloud, he remarked to Paul, "I'm glad I told Dad. It took a weight off my mind. Don't know why I didn't tell him before."

"About Brazos, you mean?" said Paul. "Me, too. I never thought any more about that old bull, until he and his partners showed up in camp. Boy, was I scared!"

Paul was shuffling along on a little sorrel

bronc, not unlike the one he rode at home, except that it was younger and more sudden-tempered. The hole in his hat was bigger, and the tuft of hair sticking through it resembled a forkful of hay.

"Scared?" said Tim. He had been scared plenty himself, but didn't like to admit it. "What of?"

"Why, you saw him kill that critter, didn't you? You ever see a fellow draw and shoot as fast as that before?"

Tim shook his head. He never had. The memory of it, combined with that other memory, of Brazos looking down at him behind the chuck-wagon with his hand touching the butt of the six-gun, gave him the old queasy twitch in the stomach again. He fought it down.

"Maybe he and the other two are just travelling," he said stoutly. "Like Dad said, they're not aiming to do us any harm."

"Maybe. Even if they are, there are enough of us to handle them."

"We'll handle 'em all right, don't worry," Tim bragged. He felt better, as he spoke. In his mind, his Dad could handle anybody. No one else rode as tall as his Dad.

"Vicente claimed the Mexican's some kind of kin to him, didn't he?" Paul queried.

"Sure. He's called Pechuga. A mighty bad *hombre*, Vicente says; killed I don't know how many folks!"

Pechuga's real name was Luis Gutierrez. Luis

had been given the nickname because he had a fondness for chicken breasts, which is what "Pechuga" means in Spanish. There was a more sinister reason as well. "Pechuga" can also mean a sickness of the chest; and a number of people had contracted such a disease from a long, sharp knife which Luis toted around with him.

The third man, Rusty Benson, was a well-known gunfighter and ruffian from Missouri, where he had served with men like Quantrill and Bill Anderson as a guerrilla during the Civil War. Undeniably brave, and deadly expert with a pistol, he was a callous brute with few decent qualities.

Wryly, Tim thought of the adventures he had hoped for when the trip began, and then remembered how bored he had been afterwards, because they had met none. By this time he was beginning to suspect that you could have too much of a good thing. When you got right close to them, gunmen and cattle-thieves were plenty exciting, but not the kind of folks you would tangle with if you had any choice.

The boys rode on for a while, until a flight of prairie grouse rocketed out of the grass in front of them. "Wish we had Tonto along," Tim said wistfully. "He'd have himself a time, chasing those chickens."

"Good old Tonto," chuckled Paul. "Pity he's too young to come with us."

"He'd be worth his place, at night time. Or any time, come to that! He's no bobcat in a fight, but you can bet nobody would sneak up on you without he'd know it."

"That's the kind you need for a watch," said Paul, who reckoned himself an authority on dogs. "One that'll kick up a racket and warn you. Not some fool that'll get itself killed by keeping quiet, and trying to make a fight on its own."

He shot a glance at Tim, and added, "You figuring we'll need a watchdog?"

Tim shrugged. "Could be. There'll be Indians around later on. Dad says they're awful slick at stealing horses."

"Indians? Will they fight?"

"Mostly they're quiet enough nowadays, Dad says. But we'll sure have to keep cases on these ponies!"

The storm, which had been rolling for days around the Wichitas, was now moving steadily out of the hills towards them. Lightning danced crazily through the heaped clouds, which were still far off as yet. Forgetting to talk, the boys watched. It was sombre and, in a strange way, very beautiful; splendid with dark majesty.

The rain hung like a curtain, miles ahead, and the air had become muggy and lifeless. Fitfully the wind died, leaving behind it a tired stillness which was heavy and oppressive.

Layton Barr riding by them at a lope, called,

"Watch out for high jinks, you big bold cowboys! There'll be something doing pretty soon."

"What d'you mean?" Paul asked.

Layton pointing to the herd, said, "They can smell the storm coming. If anything starts, leave the broncs and help look after the critters." With a wave he rode on, moving up to point to speak to Ollie.

Tim stared at the cattle, nearly always described as "*critters*". "They look kind of spooky, don't they?" he said.

"They look like I feel," Paul grumbled. "Hot and jumpy! I don't go for this weather. Feels like being in a bakery, with the oven door left open."

The steers were uneasy, becoming fidgety and hard to drive. Swing riders moved up and down on each side of the herd; they had trouble keeping the animals in line, and had to turn back steers which tried to leave the herd a good deal more often than usual.

It was a relief when camp was made a few hours later, and driving was done for the day. Cal Bryant asked Frenchy to serve a quick meal, as he expected there might be plenty to do.

"We'll work double shifts to-night," Mr. Bryant said, squatted by the fire. "The storm's going to hit us any time now, and the herd might take the notion to light out for home. I don't like the way they've been acting."

T.D.   C

The herd was very restless. Generally, after the day's journey, the steers settled down quietly to spend the night dozing and chewing their cud. Now they kept lifting their muzzles to snuff the wind, and a nagging bawl arose every few minutes, from one or another.

"They're plumb edgy, for a fact," said Layton Barr. "Wouldn't take a heap to start 'em running."

"It wouldn't," agreed Mr. Bryant. "The men on herd will have to take things slow and gentle, riding circle, and be careful not to do anything that might spook 'em. Everybody else had better be ready to hit leather right away, and take a hand if anything breaks."

"I guess there won't be much time?" asked Tim.

"There won't," said Ollie Barr, grinning at him. "Just as long as it takes 'em to make two jumps, that's all. The first to their feet, and the second to glory!"

Ollie and Layton Barr were bigger and older editions of Paul, with the same serious expression and the same fair hair. Tim looked at them in the firelight. They were lean, middle-sized, young men, deceptively slight in build, but owning a lot of strength. They were the real, old-fashioned "whalebone and rawhide" breed, able to ride or rope anything at any time, in any weather.

All the Barr boys looked as if they had just left

a prayer-meeting, and butter wouldn't melt in their mouths, but that didn't stop them from playing pranks and acting the fool when they felt like it.

Cal Bryant stood up, to glance across at the herd and then up at the sky. The clouds hung low, so that the glimmer of the fire was reflected in them. Otherwise the sky was as black as velvet, except where a clear streak of green showed low down on the horizon and threw a queer witchlike half-light across the evening.

"Tim and Paul," he said "you make sure there are enough broncs handy. Hobble them, and keep them real close to camp; there won't be light enough to see anything, in a little while. If the critters spook, there'll be no time to go hunting broncs all over the Indian Nations."

He mounted his own horse and, after giving a few more orders, rode off towards the herd. Tim knew his father would spend most of the night in the saddle. A real boss, he never spared himself when work was to be done. With the thought, Tim went out with Paul and looked to the ponies.

Later Tim was in his blankets, covered by his tarpaulin, when the first big spots of rain awakened him. They fell with slow, solid boldness, each one making a distinct noise when it landed. He listened, wondering what time it was. He and Will Dunford were to go on herd with Ollie Barr and another rider, named Lester, for the last shift.

It was so dark that he could not see anything but a faint glow from the fire, like a tiny red jewel in the enormous blackness which lay all around him. A thing passed in front of the glow and shut off its gleam for an instant. It was Ollie Barr, come to rouse him out.

"Rouse out, Tim," said Ollie. "Time to go. Better git your slicker on! You're sure going to need it."

The flurry of rain passed, and soon Tim was riding around the herd in the pitchy night. He could hardly see, although his eyes had become slightly more used to the darkness, and he let the pony wander by itself. The pony knew better than he did where to go.

Across the herd, lost somewhere in the gloom, Ollie was crooning gently. The words came across, "*Sleep tight, Baby, there'll come a glorious morning. . . !*" Tim hoped that was true, but wouldn't have given much hope of it. Thunder growled unceasingly, and the air was still so muggy that he was sweating under his oilskin slicker.

Without warning, the whole world was split in two by a tremendous explosion, dazzling him with a blue flash. In the hush that followed, the rain swept down, pouncing with a ferocity that made it seem alive and spiteful, hissing its malice.

In the swish he heard another sound. A quick, muffled thumping that grew louder in a split second. With a tight sensation in his chest, he knew that the herd had come to its feet.

The first of the two jumps!

CHAPTER SEVEN

LIGHTNING RIDE

THE SECOND jump came almost at once, whilst Tim legged his pony up to the bit. He was riding Biscuit again, and the little horse flinched at the lightning blast, dancing nervously as if he knew what was going to happen. Tim could feel him trembling between his legs.

After a solid, breathless instant, a frenzied bawl from the herd knifed through the dark. The sound was harsh and tuneless, reminding Tim absurdly of a novice trying to blow a bugle for the first time. Then, beneath the din of the storm, a swift rumble swelled.

It grew with frightening speed, loud enough almost to drown the barrage of the thunder, which now pealed without stopping. Another lightning flash hissed and crackled. Its brief glare showed Tim a wave of horns and scared rolling eyes surging towards him in a headlong flood. Then all was black again.

Biscuit spun around on his hocks as the herd reached them, and went racing into the night in the thick of a mob of bodies. The steers crowded so close that they jostled the horse, pressing against Tim's legs. Their anguished bellowing was everywhere, mingled with the clash of horns and the dull thrumming roar of their hoofs on the prairie. In the dense, inky gloom, they ran like crazy things.

It was a mad ride. Tim could see nothing, except when lightning ripped sheets of blue-white light vividly across the sky. Careering along, he and Biscuit went where the herd took them. There was nothing they could do but pelt along with the cattle. His voice cracked with strain as he yelled at the steers in a desperate effort to turn them, but he knew it was useless.

Rain beat wickedly in his face, and he smelt the thick, sweetish odour of the cattle all around him. Underneath it was another smell, like brimstone, which he supposed came from the storm.

Behind him, a good way off, he heard Ollie Barr's voice lifted high and shrill above the racket. From some place out in the dark, his father replied. He caught the words. " *Turn them!*" his father was yelling. " *Turn them*, *first chance you get . . !*"

But there wasn't going to be any chance for quite a while. Not whilst they were hitting up a lick like this!

Biscuit tore on, running like a train. Once the bronc pecked and stumbled and went down almost to his knees in a lurching dive. Fear thrilled Tim, as the cantle of his saddle lifted behind and shoved him forward. He tasted it, coming up from his knotted stomach-muscles and seizing the roots of his tongue like an electric charge, cold and awful!

The pressure of the herd alone saved them from going down. Packed densely in a crowd, the weight of the cattle lifted the pony up and onward. Biscuit had neither room nor time to fall. In a stride the pony regained his feet and lurched ahead, seeming none the worse, and again they hurtled recklessly along.

Tim hung and rattled, like a good cowhand. The lightning was still his only means of seeing anything, but the flashes were too swift for him to notice much, except the bawling, bucketing mass of animals which surrounded him. Once he caught a glimpse of a rider on his left; but, in the heavy rain, it was impossible to make out who it was.

The sight comforted him a little, knowing that he was not entirely alone in this galloping madhouse. He grew calmer, tried to learn more of what was happening. It was still pitch dark, but slowly the thunder moderated and the lightning danced farther down the sky. The worst of the storm passed.

Even so, the herd showed no signs of weakening their pace. They had lost some of the panic of their first frantic charge, but settled to an obstinate headlong run which did not falter. And still it rained.

It would be light soon, he thought. He and the others had been well into the last guard when the stampede began, so it could not be long until daybreak. He wished the time was past, with all his heart.

An age passed, before a tinge of grey filtered through the darkness. The thunder was distant by this time, and lightning blazed only rarely to the southward. A ghostly pale sheet of it lit up a steer on his left, and a man close behind it, black and glistening in the wet, and he guessed the rider was the one he had seen earlier.

The herd was spreading, showing a tendency to slacken its gait at last. Tim breathed more easily. With luck, it might end without anything terrible happening, yet! Almost unnoticed, the dawn crept out of the east, and by and by he recognised the steer which the rider was pursuing. It was Davy, leader of the herd. And the man chasing Davy was Cal Bryant!

As he watched, his father headed Davy and the steer swerved towards Tim. Instinctively Tim pulled Biscuit around, knowing what he had to do. Biscuit, game little horse, responded gallantly and went for Davy as if he was fresh from pasture, instead of having raced crazily for hours in the middle of the night. Biscuit charged alongside the steer and shouldered him into another change of direction, turned him until he was lolloping around in a circle.

"That's it!" yelled Cal Bryant hoarsely. "Make 'em turn right around! Get 'em to milling. They'll follow Davy!"

Sure enough, with some shouts and hat-waving from both of them, the front steers swerved around in their bobbing gawky lope and lumbered after Davy. More followed. The run ceased and became a shambles of trampling beasts, circling aimlessly and jostling as they went round and round.

By this time Ollie had come up, and between the three of them, they finally got the cattle halted. Davy stood for a while, panting and looking anxious. Then, with a deep gusty sigh, he nosed at the grass and tasted it.

Cal Bryant relaxed. "They'll do now," he said. "The party's over for to-day." He caught Tim's eye and smiled. "Now you can say you're a real trail hand, son. You did a good job, sticking with them the way you did."

The words made Tim feel about a mile high. He forgot the rain, and how tired he was, and the nightmare of the ride. He was a genuine cowboy now. His Dad had said so, and his Dad didn't hand out compliments for nothing!

"It sure was a mighty lively little dance, while it lasted," Ollie was resting on the swell-forks of his saddle and getting his breath. His hat was pushed back and his face ran with moisture, comically solemn. "Here's another guest, kind of late to the party."

The newcomer, whom Tim now saw riding towards them, was the other night guard, Lester. His pony limped slightly. There was no sign of Will Dunford. Lester did not know where Will was. "I never saw him or anybody, after they began to run," Lester explained, when they asked him. "I lit out after the critters, until my bronc tripped and went down. When I got up again, the poor ol' jughead was lame. I came on as fast as I could."

They saw then that Lester's side was plastered with black mud. The pony had gone down and thrown him, but he had hung on to the reins and climbed aboard again as soon as he could. A cowboy's place was with the herd, and that was where he had tried to be.

"Hope nothing happened to Will," said Cal Bryant. "We'll go look for him presently. Right now, we have to do something about the herd. Tim, you go back to camp and get the rest of the outfit here as quick as they can come. We want more hands and fresh horses, *pronto*!"

Poor Biscuit had to make another trip. The pony was about ridden right down, but could not be favoured in the circumstances. Tim sent him back along the way they had come, at the best pace he could manage. He had no trouble finding the trail, as the passage of the herd was easily read in the muddy ground.

It was nearly full daylight when he saw a figure standing on the plain waiting for him, with a saddle and gear on its head. In the rain, Will Dunford looked dejected but glad to see him.

"Boy, am I pleased to gaze on your delicate features!" said Will. "I never went a big stack on walkin', and I don't like it much better when I'm doin' it in the rain, an' totin' a saddle like a fuzztail bronc."

"What happened to your horse?" Tim queried.

Will's face darkened. He had not been as fortunate as Lester. "Put his foot in a hole, an' came down with me," he replied. "Broke a leg."

Tim nodded, knowing what Will had had to do. It was sad, but life was tough on cowponies. Will did the best thing possible, in the conditions, and put the poor brute out of its pain with his six-shooter. "Are you hurt at all?" Tim asked him.

"Only my feelings," Will grumbled. "I don't know why I ever took to herdin' cattle." He pronounced the word as "caddle". Sighing, he went on. "Sometimes I wish I'd studied to be a novelist. Then I'd have nothin' to do but set around an' make up tall tales for other folks to read. An' I'd never have to play nurse to a bunch of fool cows, or git my pants shiny polishin' a saddle."

"Likely you wouldn't eat, either," said Tim. "I heard some of your tales."

"Maybe I wouldn't," said Will. "I wouldn't be set afoot in the middle of a million square miles of rain an' mud, come to that, talkin' to a fellow about the dreary facts of life! How about givin' me a lift, Tim?"

"Hop up behind. I'll take you in to camp."

"You can do just that," said Will. "I'm kind of unsettled in my mind, and my Sunday corns ache. I was real lucky, Tim, you know that? I was way out on the rim of the herd when my bronc went down. If I'd been ridin' a yard or two to the right of where I was, them critters would have tromped me flatter than one of Frenchy's flapjacks!"

He clambered up behind Tim, who said, "Let's go. Dad needs help back there, pretty soon."

"Hold on a minute or two," Will remarked. "I want to show you somethin' before we go in. Jest head this grassburner of yours out yonder for a ways, uh?"

Something in Will's tone made Tim alert, in spite of his weariness. He forgot that he ached all over, and his thighs and haunches were cramped and stiff. As Will directed, he turned Biscuit aside and made for the spot which the cowhand indicated.

The prairie was mashed and trodden by the hoofs of the stampeding herd, and was now squashy and thick with mud. After a while they got away from the trail the steers had left, and reached clear ground. "There," said Will, pointing.

Gazing down, Tim received a shock. In the soft, untrampled earth were the tracks of three ponies.

Dunford said, "Those are the ones we were lookin' for, aren't they?"

Tim nodded dumbly. The horses which made the prints belonged to Brazos and his partners. Instead of being long gone ahead, as they had hoped, the outlaws had been close to them all the while. Without another word, he turned Biscuit and headed for camp.

And still it rained.

CHAPTER EIGHT

COMANCHES!

SOON AFTERWARDS they met the rest of the hands, pushing along fast in ones and twos. A few drove small bunches of cattle which had become separated from the rest. Tim sent them on, with a brief word as to what had happened and a warning to look out for Brazos.

Last came the chuck-wagon, with Paul and Vicente hazing the *remuda* in front of it. Quickly, Tim and Will Dunford roped fresh ponies and saddled up, then collected a handful of biscuit and cold bacon from Frenchy. Dunford loped on, munching as he rode, and Tim joined the other boys with the spare horses.

The boys pushed on as fast as they could, and left Frenchy to come behind them. There was no time to waste.

"Hope the crew gets there before Brazos starts anything," Tim stuffed the last wad of his biscuit into his mouth and spoke around it. This was poor style, perhaps, but he was in a hurry. "They were dogging us, after all. I believe they're up to no good, Paul, like you said!"

"You think they'll make a try for the herd?" asked Paul.

Tim nodded, scowling. "Looks that way. What else would they be hanging around for?"

"Our bunch should be able to handle them. After all, there are only three of them," Paul answered. He yelled at the loose horses, "Yip, yip, yip . . ! Git along, will you?"

From a little way off Vicente spoke. "Brazos got plenty men," said Vicente. "A big gang, you bet!" In the rain his straw sombrero was wilted and bedraggled, and a tiny waterfall poured off the brim on to his slicker every time he moved his head.

"How d'you know that?" Paul demanded.

"It figures," said Tim. "We haven't enough hands to drive the herd properly, ourselves; not a bunch as big as we're trailing. Most outfits have more men for a herd that size. Brazos won't do it, with only three. It's a cinch he's got others around some place, like Vicente says."

He looked at Vicente, and said curiously, "You seem to know plenty about those characters. How come?"

Vicente shrugged. "We learn from Pechuga. Pechuga, my mamma's cousin Luis, he come to see us just before we start up the trail."

"Why didn't you tell Dad?" Tim was beginning to get angry. The notion that his father's foreman would give information to a bandit seemed very bad to him.

"We not know why he come," Vicente explained, "and, anyhow, my father he not tell Cousin Luis anything much. I suppose he find out from other peoples."

"Huh!" Tim grunted. "If we find any of those *peoples* when we get home, you bet we'll make some of them plenty hard to catch!"

Still, he felt better, after hearing Vicente's side of it. He might have known that Ramon Chavez would never do anything to harm the Bryants; and it was a fact that Mexicans had a knack of getting to hear of everything, in no time at all. No one was quicker than they, when it came to finding things out.

They splashed on across the muddy prairie, driving the horses in front of them. The rain looked as if it would never stop. There was no more thunder and the hot, muggy air had cooled, but the sky sagged low and grey over their heads, without a break to be seen in it anywhere. The rain fell with a grim, steady patience which gave no sign of quitting.

It was near midday when they reached the herd. With relief, Tim saw that everything was calm. Brazos had not been up to any monkey tricks yet, at any rate.

"Good boys!" said his father. "We need those broncs right bad." He was grave, no doubt because of the news of Brazos. Added to his other troubles, it would give him a lot to think about, Tim realised. His father was stroking his moustache with one finger, as he always did when something was on his mind.

He grinned at Tim wryly, and said, "Well, this is trailing, boy! If you don't like it, you shouldn't have hired on!"

"It's all right with me," Tim protested stoutly. "I haven't complained." But he knew his father was only kidding. And, strangely enough, for all the discomfort and hard going, he knew he liked trail-droving, although it was nothing like he had expected it to be.

"Fine," said Cal Bryant and turned to Layton Barr and Will Dunford. "You boys get fresh ponies," he said, "then come with me, and we'll take a peek at those tracks. Bring rifles, and see you have enough shells."

Briefly he glanced at the steers. They were scattered, grazing quietly in the rain. "Ollie, you take over while I'm gone," he went on. "When Frenchy shows up, get a fast meal and then start them on. Don't hustle them, but don't let them dawdle, either. That run cost us a day's drive, but there's no sense in crowding more tallow off them."

Tim watched his father ride away with Layton Barr and Will Dunford. He wished he could go with them. He hoped his Dad would make out all right, and felt his stomach grip as he thought of the dozen things which might happen. A shooting, perhaps, or even——! He jerked his mind off that line of thought. His Dad could handle a dozen toughs like Brazos. It would be all right!

He and the other boys took a hand at herding, to give the others a rest. All of them were dog-tired, after the night's adventures; wet, aching and saddle-sore, and worn down with lack of sleep. Yet it never occurred to any of them to do anything but carry on with the job. A trail hand who was worth his salt put the herd before his own comfort, every time.

Frenchy Debrelle arrived with the chuck-wagon a little later, and got down to business as soon as he unhitched his team. There was no dry fuel, except a little he had in the cowhide underneath the wagon body, and he had a hard time lighting a fire. But Frenchy managed, after a couple of failures. Like most trail cooks, he knew a lot of words, and finally found the right one.

Then there was coffee, and a bite of hot food. The warm meal made them feel better, and raised their spirits. Even the rain did not seem quite so wet, after that. The meal over, Ollie Barr got the herd lined out and started north again, over the ground they had lost.

They camped before dark, near the site of their former halt. Once again there was trouble in getting a fire going. The cowchips were sodden with rain, and there was little else. It was past dark when a hail came from out on the prairie, "Hallo, there .. ! We're coming in!"

They relaxed, and Cal Bryant rode into the firelight with Layton and Will. They dismounted and stripped their broncs, brought their saddles to the fire. Tim hobbled the ponies, set them to graze near the wagon. The whole outfit kept close together these days, nobody straying farther than was absolutely necessary.

Cal Bryant shook his head at Ollie Barr's question. "No use," he replied. "We lost them again. They've had plenty of practice at hiding their sign in their business, I expect. The tracks got mixed up with those of more horses, and then the rain finished them off altogether, washed them right out."

" Other horses?" repeated Tim. Vicente Chavez's remark about Brazos having more men was in his mind. "Whose were they, Dad? Could you tell?"

Cal Bryant gave him a grim look. For a moment Tim thought he wasn't going to answer; but then, in a hard, dry tone, he said, "No point in hiding it from you, boy. You have as much right to know as the others. I think they were Indians."

"Indians!"

"That was the way it looked to us. Unshod

ponies. We found a place where one had dismounted, and he wore moccasins with heel fringes
to them."

"Comanches?" said Frenchy, looking up over
the skillet he held. His whiskers bristled as he
spoke. Frenchy did not like Comanches.

"Comanches," Cal Bryant agreed. "Don't think
there's any doubt about it."

"You figure Brazos is mixed up with 'em?" said
Frenchy angrily. "Why, the dirty renegade! I
never thought he'd git as low as that."

"Will they fight?" Ollie Barr queried.

Mr. Bryant shrugged. "Can't tell," he replied
in a flat tone. "I don't think so. They're pretty
quiet nowadays, since Quanah and Satanta came
in to Fort Sill. But they're mighty slick horse-
thieves. We'll have to watch out, or they'll be off
with our saddle stock."

He began to eat the meal Frenchy had ready for
him, and went on, "From now on we play it good
and careful. Double guards on the herd every
night, and the same guard to watch the *remuda*.
It isn't safe to put a boy alone to night-herd the
ponies, with those red comedians around. So the
boys will go on with the men, in future."

"Vicente thinks Brazos has more hands around,
somewhere," said Tim. "Pechuga told him Brazos
has a big gang."

"I expect he has," said his father. "It seems like
some of them are Comanches. But don't worry,

Tim. We'll come through, never mind what happens!"

In his blankets, Tim thought about that. He hoped it was true. From what he had heard, Comanches were plenty hot to handle.

CHAPTER NINE

INDIAN BEEF

STILL it rained.

Plodding grimly northward, they trailed the herd through the mud and wet. Twice they saw riders, watching them from a distance, but nothing happened. Suspense tightened the nerves of the crew, already rubbed raw by misery and discomfort.

Then, on the second day, the rain stopped, and the sun came out at last. Long before that, Tim had quit teasing Paul about disobeying Mrs. Barr's orders by sleeping in damp blankets. The joke was worn out.

Their clothes dried and their spirits rose. That night Frenchy was able to cook again, and gave them their first hot meal for more than sixty hours. That had been one of the worst things to bear. The ground was soaked, and there was no dry fuel. As a result, no fires could be lit, and they went without either warm food or coffee.

The next morning, they had their first meeting with the Indians. The herd was just lined out to begin the day's trip, when a group of horsemen appeared in front of them without warning. Tim did not see where they came from. At one moment there was nothing ahead but a vast, tawny emptiness of waving grass and blue sky, bright in the sunlight. In the next, the Indians were strung in a line across the path of the herd, barring its way.

Arrogantly they sat their thin scrawny ponies only a few yards away, their hard, coppery faces showing no feeling, unless it was a fierce pride. There were four of them; short, stockily-built men, with broad shoulders and broad cheekbones, wrapped in filthy blankets or buffalo-robes. They waited in grim silence, as the outfit came to a halt.

Tim noticed that they wore long fringes on the heels of their moccasins, dangling almost to the ground, and their hair and chests were decorated with silver *conchos* which glittered when they moved. So far as he could see they were unarmed, except for one who carried a short bow made of horn.

Cal Bryant rode forward, walking his pony to meet them. In response one of the Indians, a heavily-built man with a jaw like a wolftrap, and a great white scar curving down his ribs, kicked his bronc a couple of paces into the lead.

The Comanche spoke. "Wo-haw!" he said, in an explosive grunt which came from his belly. With his right hand, he began to make signs in the air.

Mr. Bryant answered, using the same method; the "sign language" of the Plains Indians. At the same time, without taking his eyes off the Comanches, he called back over his shoulder, "They want beef. Cut them a steer out of the herd, Layton . . . that mealy-nosed scalawag with the droopy horn will do."

"You aim to give 'em a critter?" Ollie Barr sounded surprised, even angry.

"Why not? It's the custom. And, anyhow, they could take plenty more, if they wanted."

"There are only four of them, unarmed," Ollie protested. "Sure we could teach 'em better ideas!"

"Do what I say, Ollie," said Cal Bryant levelly. "If there are only four here, there are plenty more within call, or I'm a Dutchman! And they'll find their weapons quick enough, if they want 'em . . . Now you go git that steer!"

Mr. Bryant kept talking with the Indians, whilst Ollie went back along the line of beasts until he found the animal which was wanted. This was a gaunt sway-backed brute, with long horns which swept downward, and a muzzle which looked as if it had been dipped in a flour-barrel. Tim recognised the steer. It was one which had given a heap of trouble all the way along the drive. Will Dunford said it had been first to run, in the stampede of a few days before.

In the meantime, Tim looked at the Indians curiously. Comanches had a bloodstained, evil name in Texas. They were the most savage and warlike of all the tribes, had raided white and Mexican settlements for years, killing and plundering. Now, seeing them at close quarters, Tim began to sense faintly what it meant to fight Indians. Their coppery features were harsh and pitiless, with no trace of weakness, the mouths shut tight and the eyes glittering like wet, black stones. In war, no mercy lay there.

Daringly, he edged Biscuit along until he was just behind his father's elbow. Mr. Bryant ignored him until Ollie Barr drove the steer towards the Indians, and then, when the savages directed their attention to the animal for a moment, Mr. Bryant said quietly, " You shouldn't have sneaked up on me, son. Can't ever be sure what these folks will do."

" Want me to go back?"

" Not now. It's too late. You never back water in front of an Indian; he's apt to figure you're scared of him, and try to take advantage."

" Why are you giving them the steer?"

" It's the custom, as I said. Most of the tribes try it on, when a herd goes through their land. Works out as a kind of fee for letting us pass."

Tim was dubious. " Will they let us through?"

His father chuckled grimly. " We'll find out in good time. I don't reckon they came here just to beg beef. More likely they're noting which ponies are the best to steal, and how we're fixed for strength."

" You mean they'll fight us?"

" Now, son, don't git any scary notions! I don't

think they'll do that; but, if they do, there's nothing to git worked up about. That won't help. We'll beat them off all right, you can bet!"

"How about Brazos?" asked Ollie Barr, who had just joined them. "You still figure he's in cahoots with 'em?"

"I hadn't forgotten him," said Cal Bryant. "He's right friendly with 'em, according to the sign we found back there. We'll ask after his health, just to see what we can learn."

Cal Bryant made more signs to the Comanche leader, who nodded and replied. To Tim's amazement, this time the Comanche spoke English. "Three paleface," he said in his grunting voice, and turned to point to the north. "Ride that way."

"How long ago?" asked Cal Bryant.

"Two sleep. Ride heap fast."

The Comanche's glance rested briefly on Tim, and it seemed to the boy that it held a spark of crafty amusement. It struck Tim then that the Indian had understood his talk with his father, and was laughing at them both. The cool nerve of it made him angry and scared, both together.

The Comanche wheeled his pony, with its mane whipping and the feathers fluttering in its tail, and looked the outfit over with a last disdainful stare. There could be no doubt that he was estimating its strength, for he took no trouble to hide what he was doing. Then he faced Cal Bryant again. "White man buffalo walk plenty slow," he said. He did not smile, but once more the sly, hard grin twinkled in his black eyes. "Too slow catchum paleface friend."

With that, he kicked the pony in the ribs and the whole bunch rode away, driving the gift steer in front of them. The very way in which they turned their backs was an insult.

"What did he mean by that?" asked Ollie Barr.

Cal Bryant chuckled again. "He says the cows walk too slow. Too slow to catch up with Brazos."

"He made out Brazos was two days' ride ahead, didn't he?" Ollie frowned, looking after the knot of riders as they herded the mealy-nose steer along.

"That's what he said, but I allow that he was lying. We know where Brazos was three days days ago. He was behind us, and it's certain he wouldn't have made that much travel in the time."

Out on the prairie there was a swift hubbub of yells and bawling. Fascinated, Tim watched. It was a barbarous sight, and made him feel queer. The Comanches had goaded the steer into a lumbering gallop and raced after it, yipping and shrieking hideous catcalls.

The man with the bow yanked a fistful of arrows from the quiver slung around his shoulder. One after another, so fast that it was like a conjuring trick, he loosed three of them into the galloping animal. The wretched brute went down, kicking and bawling, then lay still.

All at once it seemed that the prairie was full of

Indians. They seemed to spring out of the ground, yelling and thronging around the dead steer, whilst the bowman jumped off his horse and retrieved his arrows. A bunch of squat figures, which Tim realised belonged to women, began to skin and butcher the carcass.

Cal Bryant turned to look at Ollie Barr, and smiled faintly. " Only four of 'em!" was all he said. He stared briefly at the mob of Indians and back at the herd. " Ride back and tell them in the drag to close up," he said to Tim, after a moment. His tone held a dry, harsh note. " There'll be no lagging, so they're to push 'em along!" To Ollie Barr and the other point man, he snapped, " All right. Let's get going."

CHAPTER TEN

RAID ON THE REMUDA

"You suppose they'll bring us a fight?" Layton Barr knelt on one knee by the fire, mending a broken bridle with a strip of rawhide.

Busy with his camp chores, Tim listened to the men talking. At Layton's words, he cast a glance at the vast empty prairie and could not help shivering a little. Out there, the shadows filtered down and hid everything but the clean bulk of the earth against the flushed sky. Soon it would be quite dark.

His father answered Layton. "I don't guess so," said Cal Bryant, "but you never can tell. What do you think, Frenchy?"

Frenchy Debrelle was fixing some dough, ready to put in his Dutch oven to bake overnight in the coals of the fire. "Dunno," the old man snorted. "Didn't look like they were fixing to jump us, else they wouldn't have their women and kids along. Still, like yuh say, nobody ever knows what an Injun will do."

"If they come here and piroot around in the night time, they're liable to do some mighty tall jumping," promised Will Dunford solemnly. "One thing gits me real mad, it's folks racketing around and spoiling my beauty sleep!"

"Wouldn't spoil *your* sleep if they came and danced on your blankets," said Frenchy rudely. "Not unless they tromped on your face. Even then, you wouldn't wake until they jumped good and hard!"

"I'm delicate, an' I need proper rest," Will sounded hurt. For a nervous wreck, Tim thought his hands were steady as he checked the loads in his six-gun. "I suffer from acute denigration of the corollary if I miss out on my sleep, and that brings on a bad attack of inflammation of the whoozis. Then I git hysterics!"

"We'll keep a tight watch, anyhow," said Cal Bryant. "You, Tim, see that the broncs are hobbled and kept real close to camp. Whether they want a fight or not, no Comanche is going to pass up the chance to steal our ponies."

Later, just before dawn, Tim found himself riding herd. Layton Barr, Lester and Will Dunford were on guard with him. Layton and Lester were circling the beef herd, not far off, and every now and then their figures drifted slowly across Tim's sight, looking like shadows in the dark. His nerves jumped every time they showed.

To-night there was no singing to the cows. Everybody was too tense and keyed up for that;

and besides, there was no sense in a man giving away his position, if an enemy were around. The herd might be stampeded if there was an attack, but the real danger was to the *remuda*. No Indian would trouble to steal beef as a rule, if only because cows did not travel fast enough; but few would hesitate to run off a bunch of ponies, given half a chance.

Tim wore a pistol. This made him feel important, and gave him confidence. Like most Western boys of that time, he knew something about firearms, but this was the first time he had been allowed to pack a gun officially. The honour weighed on him, in more senses than one. The gun was an old Colt Dragoon Model .45, nearly as long as his arm. It was of the percussion type, loaded with powder and ball charges instead of brass cartridges, and weighed several pounds.

If he had to use it, Tim thought, he might as well dismount and lay it across his saddle, propping it in both hands. Then, if his bronc did not rise up and try to kick the stars out of the sky, he might have the luck to hit what he aimed at!

Out in the dark, the coyotes sang their lullabies. They did this every night; but now Tim strained to hear any other noise which might be hidden by their mournful yelping. The little prairie owls too were making plenty of sound. Their thin quavering hoots reached him from several directions, and it seemed to him that they were more plentiful than usual.

Will Dunford came single-footing his bronc out of the dark and reined in beside him. Will was listening, too. "Those babies sure are having themselves a time," Will remarked, after a pause. "Hear 'em sing, out there?"

"The owls? Is anything bothering them?"

"Not much, I guess. Leastways, not half as much as it bothers me! Likely they're only deciding who's going to lift which bronc, something like that."

Tim was stunned. "Indians!" he whispered at length. For the first time, he grasped what the screeching really meant. They were not owls at all, but Comanche horse-thieves!

"You can bet they're not love-birds," Will grunted seriously. "Keep your eyes peeled, Tim. I'm going to rouse out the others. If you see the least thing, holler good and loud, and loose off that Civil War field-gun of yours. Savvy?"

Tim nodded. "All right," he said, trying to keep his voice steady. "I'll do that." But Will had gone. After the cowhand left him, Tim felt a twinge of nervousness; loneliness hit him as it had never done before in his life, making him edgy and afraid.

He wished Paul was with him, for company, and he would have given anything for Tonto. Those fake night-owls would never fool the pup!

But Paul was in camp, after doing an earlier guard, and Tonto was away back in McMullen County, Texas.

Then he braced himself. Getting scared was not going to help anybody except the Indians, and the rest of the outfit would be along soon to help him.

Time seemed to stand still; the events which happened next could have taken only a few minutes, but in his imagination they went on for ages. Wherever he looked, he made sure he saw the Comanches moving in the dark. Only, when he peered hard, he found that they were only shadows. His imagination was fooling him. Small bushes, which he would not have noticed in daylight, seemed to grow tall and creep shiftily when he was not staring straight at them, like crouching men or weird stealthy beasts.

He kept close to the *remuda*. The horses were quiet, and made no noise except for a munching tear as their teeth pulled grass and, once in a while, a limping thud when they moved. Hampered by the rawhide hobbles, on their legs they could only hop clumsily a pace at a time.

Presently one of them raised its head and stared into the night, its ears cocked. Whilst the pony snuffed the air, reaching out with its muzzle, Tim felt his stomach tighten. His lips were dry, and he could not stop himself from shaking.

He squinted hard in the direction to which the horse's head pointed, but made out nothing except the slow dance of the night breeze on the grass. Closing his hand on the butt of his pistol, he drew the weapon from its sheath, his thumb on the hammer. His palm was slippery with perspiration and he gripped the gun tight.

Nothing happened. His heart lifted with a strange, dizzy excitement, which struggled with his fear. Time seemed endless. For ages he waited, but still there was no sign of movement. But the pony continued to stare.

To his surprise, the alarm came from behind him, the quarter opposite to that which he had been watching. All at once a high, shrill whoop rocketed, followed by a gunshot. A swift hubbub erupted, crazily racketing through the empty night. Then there was a wild scutter of hoofs.

Wheeling, Tim caught a glimpse of dim shapes bucketing out towards the open prairie. Forgetting his nerves, he rammed his heels into his pony, and an angry challenge pealed from his throat. He could see nothing to shoot at except the galloping shapes of the ponies, but he lifted the old gun and fired into the air. At least that would raise the camp, he thought frantically.

A man on a horse came sweeping past him. He lifted the pistol again, but Will Dunford's shout reassured him. "Stay with the *remuda*," Will yelled as he tore past. "See they don't git any more of 'em!"

Tim pulled up, forced his dancing pony around.

Of course, Will was right. His first duty was to guard the rest of the horses. On edge, he crowded them together, riding around the whole bunch and making sure that no more Indians were busy.

But the danger here was past. In the distance he heard more shots and a high owl-shrilling, followed by a shrill shriek. Layton Barr came up then, and asked, "What happened? You all right, Tim?"

"I'm all right," Tim growled. He was furious with himself, wretched because he believed he had fallen down on his job. "The Indians ran off some ponies. Will's chasing them, now!"

He still could hardly believe it. How could they possibly have got in amongst the horses like that, without being seen? But they had done it, right under his nose, and left him gaping there like a big booby whilst they got clear with the broncs!

"How many?" asked Layton.

Tim counted quickly, said, "Two. That clay-bank with the blaze face, and—and Biscuit. . . !" That hurt him more than ever. He had come to be fond of Biscuit; the little bronc and he had been through some tough times together, and the loss made him want to break down and blubber like he had done when he was small.

Running figures appeared through the dark, coming towards them. Layton swung to face them, calling in a hard tone, "Sing out!"

"All right," it was Cal Bryant's voice. "Anybody hurt?"

Tim knew relief mixed with shame as his father came close. The other hands were there too, most of them just as they had tumbled out of their blankets, but all armed. Even Frenchy was there with his game leg, holding a shotgun and snorting through his big whiskers. Frenchy was on the prod.

"They got clear with a couple of broncs," said Layton. "Will Dunford went after them."

"Will had better be careful," said Tim's father, "or they might get him, too! Comanches are nobody to monkey with any time, least of all in the dark!"

But Will showed up whilst they were talking. He was still reloading his six-shooter, his lean droopy figure black against the stars.

"Did you catch them?" Tim burst out eagerly, before it occurred to him that the question was foolish. If Will had caught them, he would have brought back the horses.

"Catch 'em?" Will repeated disgustedly. "I never even saw which way they went!"

"Oh, well," Cal Bryant shrugged. "It's no use crying over spilt milk. Nothing we can do, only kiss 'em good-bye!" Relaxing, he added, "They're gone now. Maybe they'll be satisfied with what they took, and leave us alone from now on . . . It could have been worse!"

"It could," agreed Dunford. "I wouldn't be too sure about them letting us alone in future, though, if I was you."

"Why not?" asked Cal Bryant.

Will grinned in the dark, without mirth. "I heard the horses begin to move when I was riding back after warning yuh," he said, "so I took a look-see. The Injuns were in among the *remuda* on foot, cutting the hobbles, the way they mostly do it. But there was another galoot on a horse, right close to the broncs. I thought he was Tim at first, until he pegged a hunk of lead at me."

"A Comanche?" asked Layton.

"No Comanche," Will replied grimly. "He wore a big hat and rode a shod pony, a good one. I heard its shoe clink as it hit a rock, when he ran."

"A white man?" Cal Bryant said. His forefinger came up to stroke his moustache.

Will Dunford nodded. "A Mexican," he said.

CHAPTER ELEVEN

Battle with the River

During the next few days they saw no more of the Indians. When they reached the Washita River it was bank full, swollen to the throat by the recent rains. Cal Bryant gave terse orders with a rasp in his voice, as they halted the point of the herd at the bank.

"This is going to be tough," he said. "It'll be a bad crossing; but we'll make it all right, if everybody does his best. The thing is that we're going over!"

Tim and Paul looked at the water. It was far worse than the Red had been; yellow with roiled earth and wicked in its tearing speed. Tim shivered. It seemed alive, daring them all to challenge it.

His father still talked. "Two or three of you fellows go chop down some cottonwoods and trim the boughs off," said Cal Bryant. "We'll have to float the chuck-wagon over. Frenchy, we'll hitch a couple of ropes on behind you, so we can hang on to you if you get swept away. That all right with you?"

Nothing was ever all right with Frenchy. "You think these here broncs are doggone ducks?" snarled the old man. Then he grumbled, "Make sure them *reatas* are good and tight. I don't want to end up past New Orleans, down in the Gulf of Mexico!"

A number of the hands cut down trees along the water's edge. There were not many cottonwoods big enough for the purpose, and they had to go some distance to find the number required. Then, when the boles were stripped of their branches, the trees were lashed along the sides of the wagon, to help it to float.

When Frenchy shook the lines and yelled at the team, the ponies shied. They were terrified of the racing water. Frenchy stood up, urging them on and cracking his whip until they took the plunge. The wagon went in with a great skittering splash, and keeled over to tilt drunkenly for an instant.

His heart in his mouth, Tim believed it would topple over and capsize, but the men with the ropes set their ponies to take the strain and, after a teetering second or two, the vehicle righted itself. Frenchy hauled the team's heads round to make them swim against the stream, which was so strong that they made little headway. The wagon slanted across the current, and crabbed sideways over the river with a rocking, unsteady glide.

After a battle, the swimming ponies reached the other bank, and the men cast loose the ropes. Frenchy whooped at the team crazily, urging them on. Then the animals gained a foothold and, with an effort, dragged the wagon ashore.

As before, all the hands were in their underwear, but to-day there was nothing comical about the way they looked. Or, if there was, nobody laughed. Crossing the Washita in flood was no joke.

When he saw that the chuck-wagon was safe, Cal Bryant faced the rest of the outfit. "Pony herd next," he snapped. His eyes fell on the boys, and his voice became gentler, "It's too big a chore for you young shavers to handle, this time. I'll take the *remuda* across myself."

Then he addressed Ollie Barr. "You'll boss the herd while I'm gone, Ollie," he said. "Shove them in right after me, soon as I get the broncs to swimming. I'll be back to give a hand, when I've landed the *remuda* on the other side."

"O.K., Cal." Ollie nodded, and glanced back at the massed bunch of steers. The herd was uneasy, already sensing danger, and was becoming difficult to hold. "Sooner the better, I guess. They're plenty spooky now, and they'll get worse the longer they have to wait."

Cal Bryant grinned, said, "Fine. Here's where the bathing season opens!"

With that, he drove the ponies down the bank.

They did not want to go in, and had to be hazed into the water. And then, when they were forced off the bank, the poor brutes panicked and tried to clamber out again. But they had no choice. There was no turning back, and they had to go.

In a few moments they were swimming frantically. Cal Bryant headed them upstream, as Frenchy Debrelle had done with his wagon-team; but Mr. Bryant had no ropes to help him, nothing but his own skill and determination to rely on. The horses battled against the current, churning the yellow flood wildly with their limbs, their eyes showing the whites in their fear.

The Washita swept along with a low humming growl that filled the air, carrying bushes and wrack from higher up its course. Once or twice a big tree came down, twisting and swinging like a matchstick in the grip of the river, and sailed past with unnerving speed.

Tim was worried. His father swam with the horses, which made heavy weather of the crossing and grew more terrified as the full force of the current seized them. One gave up and began to float downstream, because it was easier to swim that way.

Tim saw his father make a tremendous effort, and reach the pony before it got away from him. Yelling at it, Cal Bryant reached its head and turned it, hanging to the animal's withers as he urged it upstream again. The horses were still less than half-way across when Ollie Barr's voice jerked Tim's attention from them.

"All you boys get back to the drag," Ollie called. He was ready to start the herd into the water. "Hold the critters back there, and push 'em along after the others when the time comes. Hurry!"

Reluctantly Tim dragged his gaze from the *remuda*. There was work to be done, no more time for staring around. He gave the other boys a smile, although it did not come easily; he was still troubled about his father, wondering whether the ponies would get across safely.

Paul gave him a weak grin in reply, and he knew the other two were as worried as he was himself. No smile came from Vicente Chavez, whose face was pale under its swarthy complexion, the big dark eyes haunted. Vicente was badly scared.

Back in the drag, at the rear of the herd, there was so much to do, and the fidgeting cattle trampled up so much dust, that Tim only got rare glimpses of what went on across the river. The boys had all they could do to hold the rear-most steers together and prevent them from running, whilst the older hands pushed the main body of the herd across.

The whole scene was one of noise and commotion; bawling steers and yelling riders, with the sullen, quivering hum of the Washita underneath it all. On the bank the dust rose high, stirred up by the cattle and the bustling horsemen. It was harsh in the nose and throat, and vexed the eyes with its gritty nuisance.

Through it, Tim kept seeing fragments of the activity in the river. Steers were still plunging off the bank, urged into the water by the swing men. Half-way across, Ollie Barr was swimming with the lead-steer, Davy, and a line of bobbing horned heads straggled behind them. Other riders were in the water, moving the beasts along with hard tuneless shouts and shrieking whistles, trying furiously to keep them swimming and keep them in line.

The river boiled with the lurching and floundering of the animals, creamy patches of foam floated down with the current. The *remuda* was now almost across, but Tim could not see his father. Then he had to stop looking, in order to chase a bolting steer and head it back into the bunch. By that time the other cattle were acting up again, so he was kept busy for a while.

Hours later, the crowd of animals on the bank had dwindled, until the boys were near the water's edge themselves. Tim was tired and anxious, coated with dust and sweat like the rest of the horsemen. Eagerly, he glared at the other side of the river again.

A fair number of animals were scattered over

the grass on the other side; not spread far apart, but grazing in ones and twos, or lying down and resting. Tim's heart lifted. The worst was over now. With a bunch that size already ashore, the rest of the herd would follow. He only wished that he could see his father somewhere; if he could do that, he'd be completely satisfied.

"Hey, your Dad's over there," shouted Paul, during a brief moment when the two boys were close to one another. "See him coming out of the water, with Layton behind him?"

Tim was relieved and excited all at once. He had not seen his father, because Mr. Bryant had kept his promise and come back to help with the beef herd; after that, he was just one of the men in the water. Tim gave a shrill whoop, whacked an unruly steer across the nose with his hat and sent it back into the drag, kicking up its heels.

"Yi-yi-yi-i-i. . . !" he screeched. "Paul, we've done it! We crossed her, the mean, ugly, old Washita!"

"That so?" Paul jeered. "Look behind you, *hombre*. See if you can see any Washita-looking river back there, uh?"

As Tim was about to reply, he caught sight of Vicente Chavez. Vicente said, "Seems like Paul has something, I guess. Me, I don' see anybody across there who look a heap like us."

"Cheer up, Vicente," Tim encouraged. The

Mexican boy still looked downcast and uneasy. Tim said, "It won't be long, now. Look, only a few more to go, and then it'll be our turn!"

"Sure," Vicente nodded. "That's what scares me, plenty."

"Nothing to be scared of," said Paul. "All you have to do is hang on to your bronc, and he'll take you over."

"Maybe," Vicente sighed. "But still I git scared."

They did their best to raise his spirits, but had little time for talk. Only a few steers were left on the near bank now. These were the laziest and most fractious, and needed watching closely; stubbornly, they held back as long as they could. When the moment came, the boys crowded them in and rode their ponies into the water after them.

The river seized them like a giant hand, pulling with a crude, raw strength which was much greater than the Red had possessed. In an instant they were swimming hard, bucking the fierce current and trying to look out for the cattle at the same time.

Tim caught a glimpse of Vicente, clinging to his saddle-horn, his lank black hair plastered down in wet streaks over his forehead and his face sickly white. Paul was on the upstream side of him. Paul's eyes met Tim's, and Paul opened his mouth to say something, but his pony plunged at that moment and he got a mouthful of water before the sound came.

Then more trouble started. The last of the cattle swam in front of them. One was a big rawboned brindle animal, with horns that reached nearly six feet from tip to tip. Everybody in the outfit knew him; he was a snuffy, ornery creature, always lagging behind the herd and ready to fight any time, against cow-brute, horse or man. Without warning, the brindle steer swerved away from the rest and lunged downstream, between Tim and Vicente Chavez.

Tim cried out, and Vicente turned his bronc in an effort to reach the truant. The steer passed behind Vicente, who tried hard to head him back. Tim also went after the steer, but was too far away to catch up with it. Vicente made a frantic exertion, swam his pony right against the steer and screamed at it harshly.

An answering yell came from a point not far off. The opposite shore was now close; unnoticed by Tim they had nearly reached it. A man on a horse spurred his mount down to the water's edge, and a rope sailed through the air. The man was Cal Bryant.

With a faint hiss, the bight of the lariat settled around the steer's horns, and Cal Bryant backed his pony, pulling the steer in to land. Vicente's horse was jostling the steer, still in deep water. With a savage toss of its head, the steer plunged against the horse; unable to gore because of the rope, it charged furiously with a shoulder. The pony went under in a smother of spray. Tim had a swift glimpse of Vicente, his black eyes wide with shock and appealing for help. Then Vicente was gone.

CHAPTER TWELVE

ATTACK !

THEY NEVER found Vicente.

For two days they camped, searching both sides of the river, but no sign of him appeared. Everyone felt his loss. Vicente was well liked; a cheerful, willing worker and a good friend. His passing hit the Bryants most of all, for he and Tim grew up together, and their fathers had been friends from childhood.

"What am I going to tell his folks?" asked Cal Bryant, when there was no longer any hope. "His first trip, and that happens to him! They'll take it hard!"

"It wasn't your fault," said Frenchy Debrelle gruffly. "Jest the kind of risk that any trail hand takes. Bad luck, that's all." Frenchy's voice softened, rare for him, as he added, "He was a fine boy. He'd have made a top-hand one day, sure."

"He was a hero," said Cal Bryant, "just as much as any soldier with a chestful of medals. He was scared of water, couldn't swim; yet he went right at it, and died doing his job. The way I see it, not many folks rate higher than that!"

Sadly, they went on. They could wait no longer.

Life on the trail was hard and tough, and you had to take whatever came. On the third day, Cal Bryant said to Ollie Barr, "Point 'em north." His voice was harsh, as he added grimly, "I aim to scout ahead a little. Be back soon, I guess."

With a nod he left them, kicked his bronc into a lope. Tim watched him go, with the fringes of his old buckskin jacket whipping in the wind. Like most of the men, he was growing a beard; none of them had shaved in weeks. He sat straight-backed on the pony with his legs long in the stirrups, holding a rifle across his saddle.

Tim and Paul waited with the *remuda*, whilst Ollie and the others got the herd lined out. Ollie took his station at point, and waved them on. They drove the ponies before the herd, keeping them down to a walk. It was risky to move far from the outfit.

Although they had found nothing of Vicente Chavez, the searchers came across other signs which gave nobody any comfort. The Comanches were still around. Last night, Tim had overheard his father, talking to the two older Barr brothers and Will Dunford.

"Those Comanche bucks are dogging us," said his father. "Layton and I found their sign twice to-day."

"They don't git discouraged, do they?" said Will. For once, he was serious. "What's the tie-up, between them and Brazos?"

"Why, he's just a renegade," Layton said scornfully.

"A white man has to sink pretty low, to join Indians against his own kind," commented Ollie. "Still, it's been done, I guess."

"I've heard whispers before, that he's friendly with the Comanches," Cal Bryant told them. "Just how friendly, I don't know. Could be that he has no notion of setting them on us, of course; but I have to admit that it looks mighty suspicious."

Silence followed. Then Will Dunford growled, "Seems to me it's time somebody taught him how to behave!"

"Maybe. But it won't be us, if I can help it. Far as we're concerned, the big thing is to drive those cow-brutes to Dodge with as little trouble as possible, not to tangle with renegades or anybody else. . . . And don't any of you forget that!"

"But what if he jumps us?" insisted Layton.

"What if he does? Then we'll have to fight. But I don't see it happening yet awhile, unless the Comanches take a notion to do it on their own."

"Why not?" asked Will. "I'm still wonderin' why they haven't done it already; they had us over a barrel when we crossed the Washita. If they'd jumped us then, they'd have had us cold!"

"If the Indians do it without Brazos, it will be because they want our horses," said Cal Bryant. "Brazos wants the beef, remember. The Comanches won't help him drive it, and he can't handle it with only three men."

"So what?" asked Layton Barr.

"So he'll wait until his chances are better. I suspect his outfit's further north, and likely he's already sent them word that we're on our way. If he lets us trail on, we're droving the beef, and saving him the trouble."

"You mean they'll be waiting for us up there, some place?"

"That's it. Very likely just before we leave Indian Territory, I'd say."

"I hope you're right," said Will. "But I have a feeling those Indians are still hoss-hungry."

"If we were set afoot, it would help him," Cal Bryant agreed. "I suspect that's why he's sticking around with 'em. All he'd have to do then would be fetch his boys and take over. A couple of pistol shots, and we'd never see which way the herd went!"

The memory of the conversation ran through Tim's brain. Herding the *remuda* along, he chewed over the men's talk. If his father was right, and he nearly always was, they might not have much trouble after all; at least, not until they reached Kansas. That was, unless the Indians made a successful try at stealing the pony-herd.

The morning passed. At noon, the herd halted to graze as usual, and the riders changed ponies from the *remuda*, saddling fresh mounts. Then it was saddle-leather again, and "Walk on, little dogies!"

In the hot afternoon the grass shimmered and the wide sky was rich blue all round, except for a couple of small, woolly white clouds drifting high up. After a while, Paul said, "Don't you ever wish you were home again? No more old beans and salt bacon every meal, but decent grub to eat?"

Tim looked at him and grinned wryly. "I do sometimes," Tim admitted, "but what's the use of wishing?" He knew what was in Paul's mind. Back home, there were no Comanches either. All the same, he thought of his mother and Louise and Tonto, and wondered how they were doing. And of Ramon Chavez and his wife. Whatever happened, this drive was a tragedy for them.

"You figure those fellows are still hanging around?" Paul interrupted his thoughts.

"Your guess is as good as mine," he replied. He did not like to tell Paul what he knew. "Best to keep a lookout, anyhow."

"I'm doing that, don't you worry," Paul spoke with feeling. "They won't sneak up on me, you bet! I'm 'most cross-eyed, trying to look every which way." Deliberately, Paul squinted by way of illustration, and Tim could not help laughing at him. At best, they both were scarecrows, their clothes trailworn and ragged until they were past hope. The tear in Paul's hat, where his hair poked through, was now so big that the hat itself was nearly all hole and brim, and a battered, shabby tile into the bargain. With his serious face and his blond hair sticking through his hat-crown, and the appalling squint, Paul was the funniest thing he had seen for a long while.

The next thing he saw was not quite so funny. He did not know how, but somehow he knew they were there, even before they showed up. The grin left his face like magic, and he screamed at Paul. "Turn the horses!" he yelled, sending his own bronc around the *remuda* to drive them back towards the beef herd.

The Comanches appeared with the terrifying abruptness that was one of the amazing things about them. You never saw where they came from; they just jumped out of nowhere, right on top of you!

They were only two or three hundred yards away, coming like lunatics, their ponies skimming across the grass. As the boys turned the *remuda*, the Indians set up a high-pitched caterwauling, a quick yelping babel of hideous ferocity that made them sound like a pack of animals.

Tim and Paul sent the ponies flying back to the rest of the outfit at a dead run, hazing them as fast as they would go. The herd was a long way off. Too late, Tim realised that they had crept ahead too far, and given the Indians the chance they had been waiting for.

He thought the herd was standing still, and that his own bronc was moving like an ant across a tray of honey, so slowly that it could never reach the other side. He was never to forget those moments as long as he lived. The picture was fixed in his mind, in all its vivid urgency.

In the afternoon sun, the herd extended like a long ribbon over the dusty grass, its length trailing far back for almost a mile. The colours of the steers glowed bright in the sunshine. He saw men leave them, riding towards him and Paul in a crazy spurt.

The ponies went like birds. Their drumming hoofs kicked up a fog of tawny dust, through which he could see the goblin shapes of the Indians when he glanced behind him. The Indians were gaining.

He yelled at the horses, urging them in a voice which cracked with anxiety. They might do it yet, he thought. Yes, with luck, they could do it! Paul was on his left, screeching like a zany and fanning his pony's withers with his ragged old hat. Paul was lying flat on his mount's neck, crouched like a monkey. For once his face was ablaze with excitement as he raved at the ponies.

Then the awful thing happened.

They never knew whether the horse stepped in a gopher-hole, or what caused it to fall. The next thing Tim knew was that there was a rolling, kicking flash near him, and Paul was down.

He checked his mount instinctively, the horror of the situation freezing his heart. Wildly he glanced at the herd. It was still nearly half a mile away, and the nearest riders too far to be of any help. He swung the pony on its hocks, raced back to Paul and whirled again.

Paul staggered to his feet. So far as Tim could see, he did not seem to be hurt, but was shaken and bewildered by the fall. The pony floundered to its feet and ran on after the others, with the reins trailing and snapping around its legs.

The Indians were close now, only a few rods distant. Stridently he yelled at Paul, reached down with his right hand. Paul shook off his dizziness and grasped the hand, skipped up behind Tim with a grasshopper leap. With a double load, Tim sent the bronc after the *remuda*.

The ponies were well ahead of them, and still going like a gaggle of witches on a winter gale. Beyond the *remuda* he could see Ollie Barr flogging towards them in a boil of dust. Ollie had his pistol out but did not fire. Tim guessed he could not see well enough through the dust, and was afraid he might hit Paul or Tim himself. Someone else was coming up behind Ollie. He thought it was Will Dunford, but was not sure.

The ponies reached Ollie, who swerved around them. That cost several seconds, and the ponies were some way in front. Tim glanced back, to see where the Comanches were, because he had a bad feeling that they were pretty close by now.

He was right. An icy hand shut off his breath, made his lungs fold up with shock. Almost at his elbow rode the Comanche chief!

The old ruffian's copper face was alight with excited joy, and he was grinning broadly. The silver discs on his chest, and in his long braided hair, flashed blindingly, and the scar on his ribs gleamed pure white against his ruddy skin. Then Ollie loomed through the dust and fired.

The Comanche lifted the carbine he held and fired back. Ollie's horse went down in a tangle of kicking hoofs, kicking up another yellow cloud of haze. The Comanche whooped insanely. Then he reached out and grabbed Tim's bridle.

CHAPTER THIRTEEN

PRISONERS IN THE LODGE

THE INDIANS closed around the two boys and, holding the same breakneck gallop, wheeled away sharply to the right. Having failed in their attempt on the *remuda*, they were making sure of their prisoners.

Tim snatched a despairing glance behind him. Ollie Barr was on his feet, bareheaded by his fallen pony. The other rider was near Ollie, checking his dancing mount. The rider was Will Dunford, after all; Tim saw him plainly, now that the dust no longer spoiled his view. Both men stared after the fleeing Comanches, but gave no sign that they intended to follow.

Seeing them hold back, Tim felt an awful sinking in the pit of his stomach. Every stride of his bronc took him and Paul further away from the outfit, and the hoofbeats sounded like muffled hammering on the coffin of his hopes. Yet, even then, he realised that he could not expect anything else; the crew dared not quit the herd to chase a bunch of Indians who outnumbered them. That was asking for worse trouble than they had already!

Beyond Ollie and Will, the bunch of loose ponies had begun to halt, and other mounted figures left the herd to meet them. The herd was at a standstill, breaking up as the neglected steers drifted away to graze.

Tim had time for no more than a fleeting look, because the Indians took Paul and himself over a rise in the prairie, still racing like swallows, and the herd was lost to sight. The Indians were incredible horsemen, guiding their mounts with the sway of their bodies and handling them with beautiful skill. Both Tim and Paul had spent all their lives with horses, and could top off a snuffy bronc as well as many a professional peeler but, even in their trouble, saw that these untamed savages had few equals as riders.

The Comanches did not check their furious run for more than a mile. By then, it seemed, they felt safe from close pursuit, for they halted to breathe their ponies.

They stopped in a hollow, where the prairie folded them in a ring of grassy shoulders and hid them. At once, one of the party walked his horse up one of the slopes and paused there, just able to look over the hump of the ridge, peering back in the direction from which they had come.

The middle-aged leader turned his hard stare on the boys. Except for the crinkle of grim amusement which appeared to lurk around the corners of his eyes, his face was once again wooden and arrogant. There was no mercy in it.

"Ugh!" he grunted. The sound was explosive, jerked from the depths of his chest. "You ride with Injun. No try run, savvy?"

To make his meaning clear, he gestured sharply across his throat with the edge of his hand. With a gulp Tim decided that, if ever he and Paul took a chance on running, they had better run mighty fast.

A few minutes later, the journey began again. This time the pace was slower, although still bustling. The Comanches were in a hurry, pushed along at a running trot. From now on they kept to low ground, winding in and out of draws and gullies, and avoiding the skyline. Always they had scouts riding ahead and on the flanks, and another watched their back trail.

Nobody spoke to the boys, who were ignored except when their pony did not travel fast enough to suit their captors. Under its double load, the animal lagged once or twice. When this happened, the nearest buck gave it a crack with the end of his rawhide rein, or the braided quirt which hung from his wrist.

Riding behind Tim, Paul was out of luck. Either through sly malice or through carelessness, the Indian was not always particular where the blow landed, and Paul got the benefit of it.

They rode all through the afternoon without stopping, except for a halt now and then to ease the horses. By dusk they had travelled nearly twenty miles. Then, as the red sun died, they dismounted at last on the banks of a little creek, fringed with cottonwoods and willows.

The boys were allowed to drink from the creek, but were given no food. They were then tied with rawhide thongs, so securely that they could not move. When they tried to speak to each other, they were told roughly to be quiet.

No fire was lit. The Indians merely wolfed a few strips of "jerky", or dried meat, tearing the leathery stuff with their teeth and bolting it. When they had eaten they all lay down and slept, but for a sentry who watched by the picketed ponies.

The boys spent a poor night. Used to rough living, and hardened as they had become by life on the trail, they had never known such discomfort as this. The hide whangs bit into their muscles until the ache was unbearable, and they could do nothing to ease the cramps. But they knew better than to complain; a protest might have led to something worse.

Yet the physical hardship was not as bad as the dark thoughts which attacked them. Both wondered what lay in store for them; they had heard ugly tales about the Comanches. They did not even dare to speak to each other, and try to gain some comfort from that.

And then there was the worry of thinking about

their folks. Tim kept remembering his father, and imagining his distress when he heard the news. Ollie and Layton Barr, too, must be hard hit by the loss of Paul. And then there were the others, back in Texas. The Chavez home was not the only one which was going to get bad news, it seemed. There was not much hope that either Paul or himself would ever see their friends again.

Somehow they got fitful snatches of sleep, as best they could. Numbed with cold and cramp, they were awake before the Indians stirred, long before dawn. The squat body of the chief loomed suddenly above them against the paling stars, appearing out of nowhere like a ghost. With one of his chesty grunts, he loosed their bonds. For a minute or two he let them flex their limbs, watching with something like contempt, as they grimaced and flinched at the pins and needles which ran through their stiffened flesh.

Then the ponies were untethered. The boys had to mount double again, and were tied to the horse. Almost at once the whole band was away, heading southwest as they had done before.

By and by the sun came up and warmed them, shining down on them cheerfully as they jogged across the tawny lion-coloured prairie. The grass was high and grew in bunches, the tufts bowing in shimmery waves as the breeze played over them. All around, as far as they could see, there was nothing but grass.

About half-way through the morning, a sound pierced the gloom which had settled on Tim's mind. Absently he put it down to coyotes at first; but then, as it went on, he knew he was mistaken. Coyotes did not bark like that; their note was higher and more savage, and mostly they only gave tongue at night. The barking was made by dogs.

He was right. Soon they rode over a lip of ground, to look down on a hollow in the plain; a wide shallow basin, through which flowed a creek. All along both sides of the water stood an untidy huddle of lodges, with tanned buffalo-hide coverings warm in the sun and painted with red and black symbols.

The dogs in the village were now raising a great hullabaloo, and people swarmed between the *tipis*, staring at the newcomers. A knot of riders broke away from the village and came tearing up the slope, urging their ponies to full speed and shrilling at the tops of their voices.

When they came closer, Tim and Paul saw that most of these were youngsters, some of whom were boys smaller than themselves. The young Comanches performed all kinds of agile feats on their ponies, giving themselves airs and cutting a dash.

The grim old leader of the homecoming party paid little heed to them, apparently because it was beneath his dignity. Except for a few short words in reply to their greeting, he ignored them and rode on down to the lodges without looking at them again.

His companions adopted the same pose; staring ahead and acting as if they had not been anywhere much, except perhaps for a half-hour pleasure trip around the camp. Only the swell of a bare chest here and there, and the proud lift of a chin, hinted that they thought themselves pretty important fellows.

The gang of youths jostled about the party on their trampling broncs, making the horses throw their heads and snort in nervous excitement. They pressed close against Tim and Paul, giving the boys fierce stares and crowding them rudely.

Hunched behind Tim, on their single mount, Paul dared to whisper in his ear, "Watch these babies, *hombre*! Heap bad medicine!"

"Shut up," retorted Tim. He muttered, without moving his lips: "Take no notice of 'em. Don't let 'em think you're scared!"

"Who are you trying to kid?" Paul hissed. "I'm shaking like a wet pup, just come in out of the rain . . . And I can feel you twitching plenty, too!" But he shut up after that, all the same.

By then they were splashing through the creek, heading for the centre of the camp. More folks came to gaze at them, thronging between the lodges. The men only stared in grave silence, but the children and squaws jabbered and squealed in welcome. The barking of the dogs mingled with their voices to create a deafening racket.

The prisoners came in for a lot of attention. More hostile stares were directed at them, and the triumphant squeals from the women and children did nothing to soothe their nerves. However, they were not molested, and had to ride with the party as chief exhibits in a victory parade around the camp.

Finally they reached a group of lodges, outside the biggest of which the chief reined in and slid off his pony. His wife and several children waited for him there, but he ignored them and went inside the big lodge. Later, the boys found out that Indians could be as affectionate to their families as anybody else, but their code of manners was against a show of feeling in public.

Tim and Paul waited outside the *tipi*, still tied on the horse, until some of the youths unbound them and pulled them down. At that point the chief came out again, and gave some orders in a quiet deep voice. The youths hustled the captives to a smaller lodge, which stood behind the others, whilst the chief strolled calmly after them.

The boys were bundled into the lodge, and the youths stayed outside, moving away from the entrance to let the chief come in. He looked down at them gravely, puffing at a Mexican *cigarillo*. For all the world, thought Tim bitterly, like a dignified old gentleman sizing up a pair of colts he had just bought!

After a pause the chief removed the cheroot and spoke. "You stay in lodge," he said. "No go out. You go out, plenty trouble."

They did not answer. He regarded them calmly for a minute, then cast an eye around the lodge; there was not a thing in it, except themselves. As if satisfied, he nodded. "Bimeby eat," he said. "You wait."

With that, he turned and went outside.

CHAPTER FOURTEEN

War Chief

"What will they do with us?" asked Paul.

"No savvy," Tim answered. He tried to keep his voice even, as if he believed it did not matter very much. "Maybe they'll try to sell us back to our folks for a ransom. I've heard they do that, sometimes."

"How long d'you figure it'll take?"

"A pretty good while, I guess." It might even be a longer time than that, Tim thought; he couldn't remember where he had heard that Comanches ransom their captives, and had only said so to make Paul feel a little better. But it was no use worrying about it.

Now that the sensation had come back into his muscles, after being untied, he rose and moved to the entrance of the lodge. There was no harm in taking a peek outside, he told himself. There was nothing much to look at in here. Except for himself and Paul, the only thing the lodge held was a mixture of several smells. The odour was not bad; a kind of smoky, musky, leathery flavour, which he recalled having noticed on the bodies of the Indians who captured them.

The flap at the entrance was shut, but he pushed it aside and poked his head through the opening. At once a shadow blocked out the daylight, and a figure stepped in front of him. The sentry was one of the Comanche youths, who now carried a club which he raised with a fierce gesture. Tim stepped back quickly, as the youth pointed with his free hand, telling him to get inside the lodge again.

"What's eating him?" growled Paul in a low tone. "The mean ugly critter!"

"My guess is that he doesn't want us to go outside. I expect he has orders about us."

"Orders or not, he don't need to act up so tough and ornery. If I had him by himself, without his folks around, I'd teach him how to treat visitors real polite!"

"Only thing wrong with that is, his folks are around," Tim said. "If you started anything, they'd come a-running, you can bet that scarecrow old tile of yours!"

However, the sentry did not close the flap again, and they were able to see something of the Indian village from where they sat on the ground. Plenty was going on. Smoke lifted from fires, and people moved about their business. Squaws were cooking, or carrying out other tasks; one, not far away, was scraping a hide which was pegged out flat on the ground, and others fetched water and bundles of firewood from the creek.

Children played and dogs scavenged. Outside some of the lodges, a lance had been set in the ground, and trophies hung from it. This meant that the owner of the lance was at home. Often the warrior sat outside, combing his long black hair with a bunch of porcupine quills, and braiding ornaments into it. They were very fond of flashy decoration. Generally this consisted of silver or bright metal, with feathers, beads and sometimes pieces of glass. Anything would do, so long as it glittered and made a show.

Ponies, too, stood outside the lodges, hitched ready for use. A number of them were visible from the spot where the boys squatted inside the *tipi*, and watched. Looking at one of them, Tim gasped suddenly.

"Something wrong?" Paul asked quickly.

Tim pointed. "I'll be a son of a gun!" he exclaimed. "See that bronc, past where the fellow with the big nose is tying doodads into his hair?" Tim, angry and excited, forgot the danger they were in. He shouted, "It's Biscuit! And that buck must be the thieving polecat who stole him!"

Sure enough, Biscuit was tethered outside a lodge where a warrior with a big Roman nose was fixing some polished harness brasses into his twin braids of hair. Biscuit looked thin and gaunt, as did most of the Indian broncs. Indians worked their mounts hard, and got a lot more out of them than white men did.

"Nerve!" growled Paul. "Sitting there as cool as all git-out, and fussing with his hair like a girl. I wish our boys could just see him, now!"

"I wish they could see us," said Tim glumly. "Then maybe we could get out of here." His voice quickened, and he added, "Looks like that squaw's heading this way. I think she's bringing us some grub."

The squaw entered, after a few words with the guard outside. She did not speak to the boys, however, only stared at them with blank dislike, and held out the food she had brought. They took it from her with a mutter of thanks, and she turned and went out again with the toe-in shuffle all the women had.

The meal was not brilliant, even by trail standards. It was no more than two lumps of unidentified meat, each skewered on a stick, and partly cooked. The parts which were cooked were nearly black, and the rest was raw. But they were starving, and in no mood to turn up their noses at anything that could be eaten.

Holding the sticks, they chewed at the meat, charred pieces and all, whilst they gazed out of their prison. When they had done, they wiped their greasy fingers on the grass, having no other way of cleaning them.

Both of them dwelt on the future, in their own minds. To Tim, it did not look good, but it had to be faced. Suppose the Indians did not ransom them, what then? Like most Westerners of his time, he knew plenty about Indians.

The Comanches had been a scourge to Texans for generations. After a long and bloody struggle, with no quarter on either side, they had finally been broken as a fighting nation, most of all by General Mackenzie's victory at Palo Duro Canyon. Later, ragged and starving, their great chief Quanah Parker brought in the last remnants of his force and surrendered, at Fort Sill.

But they were still wild and intractable, capable of breaking out again if they felt like it. Comanches did not like being pushed around. Tim believed that their captors would have to give them up in the end, but there was no certainty of it; in any case, it might take a long while, and life was not going to be a bed of roses in the meantime.

He wondered what his Dad was doing. "I guess the outfit will go on," he said aloud. "They can't afford to stop for us."

Paul nodded gloomily. "They can't leave the herd," he agreed. "Don't know what they could do, anyhow. We're a long way from them now, even if they could trail us."

"Expect Dad will see the Indian agent at Fort Sill," Tim spoke more hopefully than he felt. "The agent will make 'em behave, you bet." He was looking out of the lodge as he spoke. The Indian who now owned Biscuit was fitting weasel skins over the ends of his twin plaits of hair, to make a dandy finish. Behind him, other figures came into sight. Tim's heart gave a little jump, and he whispered hoarsely, "Watch out, *amigo*! We're having visitors!"

Paul was with him instantly. Paul whistled. "So he was with them after all," he breathed. "The dirty renegade!"

Brazos and the Mexican, Pechuga, walked with the chief who had led the raiding party against the herd. The third outlaw, Rusty, was missing. The men entered the lodge and squatted. Brazos and Pechuga grinned at the boys, but the chief ignored them.

"Howdy," said Brazos. "You kids sure git around, don't yuh?"

They did not answer him. He chuckled, and turned to the Indian, beginning to speak in a mixture of English, Spanish and sign language. It turned out that the Comanche spoke Spanish better than English, and the boys were able to follow the talk without much trouble.

"How much do you want for the boys?" Brazos asked.

Tingling with suspense, the two youngsters listened. The question aroused their hopes to fever pitch; much as they disliked and feared Brazos, they were eager to become his prisoners, rather than remain captives of the Indian.

"I had not thought of selling them," was the

reply. "Maybe, if I keep them, they will grow into good Comanches and become my sons."

"Those days are over," said Brazos. "If you try to keep prisoners now, you will be in trouble with the agent at Fort Sill."

The Comanche's opinion of the agent was evidently low, for he used a rude word to dismiss him from the conversation. "If the Pony Soldiers from the fort will take them from me, as you say," he answered coolly, "why do you wish to buy them? They will be free then, and cost you nothing. Perhaps you want to take them there, and sell them at the Fort? That way you make a profit, uh?"

"They are of my people," protested Brazos, his doggy smile no longer visible. He was serious, now. "It is natural that I should want to send them back to their families. Even if I make a profit, what is wrong with that? You will still make money or guns, whatever you ask. If you wait for the agent to hear about it, you will get nothing."

"We shall see," said the Comanche. He was smoking again, puffing on the brown roll of tobacco without any sign of emotion. A moment later, he said, "Your friend with the sorrel hair has ridden from my village. It is said that he has gone to tell the soldiers that we have the boys."

"That is not so. Rusty has gone north. Fort Sill lies south of here, as you know."

"I hope that is true," said the old man calmly. "Because, if the soldiers come here to look for them, they will find nothing. They will not even find two men they have been trying to catch for a long while."

Brazos said nothing, but his face was wicked. He glowered as the chief rose and said, "The talk is finished. You can stay and talk to the boys, but after that you must leave them alone. Those are my words."

He went out, leaving the whites. After he had gone, there was silence for a while. Brazos drew a long breath at length, and said, "You boys are in a tough spot. The old son of a gun won't let you go, unless he can be talked around."

"Why does he want to keep us?" Tim asked. He was scared, but tried not to show it.

"Just plain mule-headedness, mostly," said Brazos. "He was a war chief under Quanah, but didn't want to come in when the others did. He's in two minds whether to break out again and hit the trail, to show the white man he still isn't licked."

"I don't aim to become any kin to a dirty old savage like him," Paul burst out. "I'd die first!"

Brazos gave Paul a long queer stare. "It's up to you, son," he drawled at length. "You can take your pick. Because if it works out like that Injun wants it, you'll likely do one or the other."

CHAPTER FIFTEEN

LEADER OF THE WASPS

TIM could not hold in his anger any longer. "It's your fault," he cried. "You're behind it all!"

Brazos looked at him for a long while, with the hard, brilliant stare he had. The dark eyes burned with little hot flames that seemed to dance. Then Brazos smiled, but it was not quite the reckless dangerous grin they had seen before.

"You're way off your target," said Brazos. "They'd have come after your ponies anyhow. I had nothin' to do with that."

"Then why was Pechuga with them, when they stole Biscuit and the other horse?" Paul challenged.

Brazos and the Mexican exchanged glances. Pechuga cleared his throat politely, and after a shifty pause, said in Spanish, "Of what are you talking, *Señorito Barr*? Surely you do not accuse me of being a common horse thief?"

"No," Tim snapped. "We think you're out of the common. Only black renegades would help Indians to raid and thieve!"

"You can't prove he was there," challenged Brazos.

"He was seen," said Tim, "and his tracks found

later. Besides, we knew all along that you were with the Comanches."

Brazos pulled at his thin moustache. "We met up with 'em on our way north," he said. "I do business with 'em sometimes. It just happened that we tagged along with 'em, that was all. When they took a notion to make a play for your *remuda*, there was nothing we could do to stop 'em."

"I bet you tried hard!" sneered Tim.

"All right," said Brazos. "Let's say we were with 'em. But, if you savvy Comanches, you know they take orders from nobody. They please themselves what they do, an' if anyone tries to stop 'em, it's Katy-bar-the-door. You heard that old rascal tell me and Pechuga we'd overstayed our welcome around here? Well, that was because I tried to buy you from him. Now he's gone back to his lodge, to figure out whether he'll rub us out or not."

"Who is he, anyhow?" Tim asked, still unconvinced.

"He's a Number-One war-leader around here, kid. Big chief of the Wasps, which is the tribe this outfit belongs to. Far as I can make out, he has an Indian name that's somethin' like 'He who strikes many enemies '; but most whites call him ' Coup-Counter '."

The boys were startled into a fresh thrill of disquiet. They had heard of Coup-Counter. Most

Americans had; he was famous. It was Coup-Counter and his band who fought several pitched battles with Federal cavalry in the Staked Plains, and came off best every time. He was notoriously cruel and savage in war, even by Comanche standards.

"How did you come to know him?" Tim asked, at length.

"Like I said, I've traded with him sometimes. Mostly buying cattle. But that don't mean he likes me; if he takes the notion, he'll try to kill me as quick as you can yell ' Mama!'."

"You mean you had nothing to do with him kidnapping us? Honest?"

"Cross my heart," replied Brazos, wearily. "That's what I'm trying to tell yuh! I've done some pretty tough things, but I don't go for a deal like that, ever."

Easily Brazos got up, moving with the suppleness of a lazy cat. "Me and Pechuga will have to git out of this camp, if we can," he told them. "It ain't safe for us to hang around any longer." He hesitated, as if not liking what he had to say, then added gruffly, "If we can do anything to help yuh, we will; but don't count on it too strong. Best thing is for yuh to play along with 'em as much as yuh can, an' try to keep out of trouble. But keep your peckers up. Maybe yuh'll git a break!"

With that, he left. Pechuga paused at the

entrance flap of the lodge and turned to look back at them. There was genuine regret and sadness in his face. "You got plenty sand, both," he said. "*¡Vaya con Dios, amigos, y buena suerte!*"

The flap quivered, and they were gone. Both boys were silent for a while. Then Paul muttered, "Do you believe what he said?"

"About trying to help us? I think he was telling the truth."

"I hope they can fix something," said Paul gloomily. "We sure need all the help we can round up. What you figure they'll do?"

Honesty made Tim confess, "I can't see what they can do, except save themselves. It'll take them all their time to get clear, without trying to monkey around and help us."

Another silence followed. "Maybe he'll send word to Dad, if he gets away," Tim said at length, "or to the agency. They'd send the cavalry after us."

"Brazos wouldn't dare try the agency," replied Paul. "If he showed up there, the cavalry would nail him. They've been looking for him for years, you know that."

"He could still get a message through," Tim contended. "I believe he will, too, if he can. But, either way, it looks to me like we shall have to make a break ourselves, if we aim to get away."

"Say, you think we could?" Paul's eyes lit up. Then his face fell, and he accused, "You're only saying that so I'll feel good. You don't really think we'd make it."

"If I had Biscuit, I'd sure give those ugly sons a run for it. Maybe we could snake a couple of broncs out in the night, and pull out."

"Yes. Maybe we could grow wings and fly, too!" Paul was bitter. "I can see 'em leaving broncs around, where we can get to 'em."

Tim stepped to the door, but not too close, in case that fellow with the club busted him one. Outside nothing much was happening. Brazos and Pechuga were standing outside the lodge of Coup-Counter, talking to him. The Indian sat there with his blankets around his loins, and looked through them; so far as the Comanche was concerned, they did not exist.

Seeing that it was useless to linger, Brazos shrugged and walked away, with the Mexican following. Pechuga glanced back as if casually, and saw Tim inside the tent. Tim saw him lift his shoulders, almost imperceptibly, and shake his head.

It was no use, then. Glum and sick at heart, Tim went back into the lodge and sat down. "Don't take things so hard," Paul told him. "I guess those two lilywhite babes will do something, anyhow."

Tim said nothing. It would not help to tell Paul that, if Brazos was able to do anything, it was going to take an awful long time.

The day wore on. Just before dusk, the guard led them down to the creek and let them wash and take a little exercise. Evidently he had orders to keep the rest of the crowd away, for he swung his club importantly when the other hobbledehoys pressed too close.

The boys went back to the lodge, feeling slightly refreshed. On the way, they saw the Comanche pony-herd driven close in to the camp and picketed. Tim noted that Biscuit and the claybank pony, which the Indians had stolen from his father's outfit, were now with the rest of the herd; probably the horses would be well guarded, during the night.

Inside their prison the chief, Coup-Counter, was waiting. Iron-mouthed as always, he said harshly, "Your friend say he buy you from me; many ponies, many guns. I no sell!"

As they looked at him, his face appeared to soften. "You good boys," he continued. "Stay with Coup-Counter. I no have son now; white soldiers killum two son. Now white men give me back two son! You be good Injun bimeby, fight soldiers."

They did not answer. In spite of that, they managed to give him back look for look, scared though they were of him. He was not displeased, and added, "The white man and the Mexican are in my lodge. They stay there now. If they try makum fight, I kill. Savvy?"

Tim nodded. Realising that Brazos and Pechuga were in much the same boat as Paul and himself, he was sorry for them. So far as he could gather, he and Paul had a chance of at least a tolerable existence, if they did what Coup-Counter wanted; but things looked black for Brazos and Pechuga. Their lives hung on the whim of this old savage.

Coup-Counter stayed whilst the Indian youths bound them. The Comanche was taking no chances on them trying to escape. They were bound securely, their arms behind their backs and their ankles hobbled, so that they were scarcely able to move. Then they were left alone.

Dark came. Gradually the camp noises died, except for the snort of a pony now and again, and the baying of a dog in reply to the coyotes' singing. The coyotes yipped all around, mournfully dismal, and added to their dejection as they listened.

They could not sleep. To Tim the night was endless, the black minutes dragging by like months. The flap at the entrance was closed, and not even a glimmer of starlight filtered in to relieve the pitchy dark.

"What time is it?" whispered Paul, after an ageless time had crawled over them.

"Dunno." Tim supposed it was somewhere around midnight, but could only guess. Lying there, in that inky gloom, there was no way to find out. "Must be late," he said. "Why don't you sing out and ask the Comanches? They'd be glad to tell you."

"Funny, aren't you?" sneered Paul. "I bet Comanches don't know how to tell time, anyhow. Come to that, it's about as much as you can do to tell it yourself! Only when your insides ring the grub-triangle."

"You aren't so hot, either. If you were, you wouldn't have asked me!" Tim growled. "What difference does it make? We have all the time there is!"

"I'd swap a piece of it for an hour or two on a goosefeather bed," Paul retorted. He was going to add something else, but checked himself and muttered swiftly, "Listen. . . !"

Sprawled on the grass floor of the lodge, they lay with their ears alert. For a space nothing happened, and Tim was just going to ask what Paul had heard, when a faint sound reached him. It was a fleeting rustle, on the other side of the buffalo hides which comprised the wall of the lodge; so slight that he was not sure he had not imagined it. It resembled the stealthy creep of a dog, he thought, or perhaps a coyote, skulking around the village on the lookout for offal.

Then his nerves froze. Without warning, a slit opened in one of the hides, running downward in the lodge wall. Tim stared as it widened, and a thing slid through it quickly. He began to shake. What was this? For he knew the thing was a man, and the first thing that came into his head was that it was one of the Indians, come to do them a mischief.

Near him, Paul's breath sobbed in dry gasps, and he knew that Paul was as scared as himself. Tied as they were, they could do nothing to defend themselves. They were helpless!

CHAPTER SIXTEEN

RACE FOR LIFE

BREATH SIGHED warm on Tim's cheek. In his
ear a voice sounded, low and quiet, the words so
soft that he barely heard them. "*¡Cuidado!*" the
voice murmured. "Be careful! No make the noise,
please."

Hands fumbled for the thongs which bound
Tim's ankles and, after some swift meddling, the
rawhide cord slackened and fell away. The hands
caught him and turned his body over, and bare
steel touched the flesh of his wrists, sawing
through the bonds which held them. His head
whirled as he got up. He was free!

"Wait," breathed Pechuga. "In one minute,
we git you out of thees kennel. But make plenty
quiet, uh?"

More fumbling took place. Then Paul climbed
to his feet and cannoned into Tim. Tim grabbed
him and held him, guessing that his limbs were
numbed with cramp, and he could not stand
properly. Pechuga brushed past them and slipped
through the gash in the wall, after peering out
to make sure that all was quiet.

The boys crawled after him and stood outside the lodge, cringing in its shadow. After the chimney-black darkness which they had left, the night was luminous and pleasant; there was no moon, but the starlight and the clear sky helped them to adjust their vision.

The pale skins of the *tipis* gleamed faintly, with a bloom of almost unearthly calm. There was not a sound anywhere, except a light breeze which wandered through the brush along the creek. The whole world slept. Under the enchantment of the night, the boys were rigid with excitement and suspense, held by the eerie magic of the adventure.

With an awful shock, the spell was broken. A figure emerged from the shadows and stole around the lodge where they crouched, coming towards them. Dim and ghostly, it loomed in silent menace.

Paul clutched Tim's sleeve in a shuddering grip, his fingers digging into the flesh, but Tim hardly felt him. Tim could only stare. Anger and despair filled him, at the thought that their escape was finished already. A crazy notion seized him, and he half made up his mind to take a dive at the Indian, and try to hold him whilst the others ran.

Then, close to weeping with reaction, he saw that the Indian was Brazos!

Brazos was smiling. His teeth glinted through

the dark, and Tim knew that the old doggy grin
was back there. Brazos murmured, "Hit for the
creek, boys. Watch out where yuh plant your
great hairy hoofs, an' try not to make any more
racket than yuh have to, uh?"

His left hand carried several coils of line. With
his right, he beckoned them to follow Pechuga,
who was scuttling towards the inky line of timber
which grew thick on the banks of the stream.
They set off behind the Mexican at a run, doing
their best to keep quiet.

In the shelter of the willows they stopped to
listen, crouching and holding their breath. The
water ran past their boot-soles with a gentle
chuckle and the night wind rustled the leaves,
but there was no other sound. Not even a dog
yelped in suspicion.

Staring at the village, Tim watched the dream-
ing lodges; nothing stirred there. Everything
was utterly still. His eye wandered past the lodges,
and beyond them he made out a shadowy mass
out on the plain. After he gazed at it for a
little, it showed vague unrest, and he knew
what it was. The Comanche horse-herd grazed
there.

Brazos pointed to the herd. "We have to git
down there and grab us some broncs," said the
outlaw under his breath. "There's a young buck
night-herding them. We'll have to sneak up on
him without letting him hear us." Brazos

paused, and added grimly, "Yuh know what'll happen if we botch it, don't yuh?"

There was no need to answer. All of them knew. With no more talk, Brazos glided down the bank and stepped into the creek. Stealthily he began to wade down the bed of the stream, keeping close in under the willows.

Creeping like rats, they followed him. The water was cold, flowing around Tim's thighs, and he shivered as much with nerves and suspense as with the chill of the current. He recognised the cunning of Brazos, in going about the job this way; any slight noise they made would be covered by the ripple of the water flowing, and they were low down, so that no one could see them against the sky.

Ducking beneath the overhang of the willow branches, they made their way in single file until they reached a place near the horses. This was as close as they could come, without leaving the creek. Here Brazos checked them by turning the flat of his hand behind him, without speaking.

Again they listened, but heard nothing. Brazos made another sign, and Pechuga joined him. Side by side, he and the Mexican lay on the bank for a minute, peering over its edge through the brush. Then, with a wriggle, Pechuga glided away like a rattlesnake and lost himself in the undergrowth.

The boys could not resist the urge to see what went on. No slouches at moving quietly themselves, when it suited them, they crept up on to the bank and went flat on their bellies.

Gazing through the starlight, Tim found that they were only a few yards from the group of horses. The ponies were bunched together in a loose crowd. Some were stretched out on the ground, and others stood with their heads down in a doze, or sleepily cropped the grass. He could not see the Indian herder.

At that moment, one of the ponies lifted its head and turned its nose towards them. Softly it blew through its nostrils, in a gusty snort, and raised its head higher with its ears pricked. Immediately several others imitated it, until the whole bunch was alert and curious.

Half crazy with impatience, Tim wondered why Brazos and the Mexican did not act at once. In another moment it would be too late, and their chance would be gone! No Indian was likely to ignore the restless behaviour of the horses. Tautly he expected the herder to come over and find them, and then raise the camp. But Brazos lay close, waiting, and kept still.

A few yards upstream, where the brush grew low and dense, foliage rustled and a coyote yipped. That made matters worse. Pechuga must have disturbed the creature, Tim thought bitterly. Now the fat was in the fire altogether!

That was when he saw the Indian herdsman. The Indian was there, right in front of him, staring into the brush. Tim had not seen him come. The Comanche stood quite still, his head sunk forward slightly; there was a bow in his hand, half drawn, with an arrow notched to the string.

He was staring straight at Tim. For a long while, he glowered into the undergrowth, keeping so still that he was almost invisible even though he stood out against the sky. It was a knack these people had; a gift of losing themselves simply by blending with their surroundings, so artfully that the eye was deceived.

Tim recognised the herder. He was the youth who had threatened them with the club, when he guarded them in Coup-Counter's lodge. It seemed to Tim that the youth knew he was there, because they were gazing into each other's faces, and he couldn't understand why the Indian did nothing about it. But the youth drifted away at last, and some of their tension relaxed. He had not seen them, after all.

The youth skulked on up the bank, towards the patch of brush where Pechuga had disturbed the coyote. Again he stopped, and a figure pounced from the dark behind him. Sensing its presence by instinct, the young Comanche whirled swiftly, but was not quite fast enough.

Brazos was on him before he could cry out.

Brazos clapped a hand across the herder's mouth, gripping him so tight that he could not get clear. At the same time Pechuga jumped out of the willows and joined in, the three of them grappling in vicious silence.

The struggle did not last long. Soon the herder was on the ground, and the two men tied him as they would a calf at branding-time. Gagged with his own breech-clout, the youth lay writhing as Brazos straightened and looked down at him. The Indian battled in futile rage against his bonds, the pigging-strings which every cattle-hand carries, and with which his captors had tied him.

Shoving back his hat from his forehead, Brazos drawled, "Well, that ought to hold him for a spell. Now let's go git those cayuses, we stayed around here too long already!"

He picked up the ropes which he had dropped in the bushes, and handed one each to the boys and to Pechuga. They were Comanche *reatas*, supple rawhide nooses that handled neatly. "Go grab one each," he said. "Hurry!"

The ponies shifted nervously, but did not run when they approached at a gentle walk. Tim had already marked out Biscuit for his prize. No Indian was going to hold on to a bronc that belonged to his outfit, while he could prevent it. The ponies scattered as they made their throws, but there was no great confusion.

Tim's rope settled on Biscuit and he went along it hand over hand whilst the pony snorted and backed away, throwing its head in alarm. He spoke to it, soothed it in a gentle murmur, and it let him get a grip on its mane. With a jump, he was astride its back.

The others were mounted too, and the *remuda* was now fully aroused, timidly prepared to run at any instant. Sitting on Biscuit, Tim knew a wild elation. It was as if a huge weight had rolled from his spirit; a great stone which had crushed it down, and now fell away to let it surge up again. He wanted to shout in his exultation.

Brazos's voice came to him. " Watch out, they're awake yonder!" He was about to kick his heels into Biscuit's flanks, when the outlaw went on in a sharp tone, " Run the other horses off. We don't dare leave them a mount, or they'll be after us like hornets!"

As Brazos had said, there were sounds among the lodges by this time. Indians sleep light, and the fidgeting of the pony herd had aroused them. Yells and angry questions pierced the darkness, and figures began to run from the *tipis*.

A faint twang, like a flat guitar string, floated to them, followed by others. Tim was busy, helping to bunch the horses, when something buzzed close to his cheek with a spiteful whisper. More arrows zipped around the fugitives, quiet and humming wickedly.

"Now!" pealed Brazos, "Fog it out of here. . . !"
The crash of his six-gun split the night in a ragged
blur of noise, and he whooped at the top of his
voice. The yell was derisive and triumphant.

Then they were going flat out.

CHAPTER SEVENTEEN

ON THE RUN

PECHUGA RAMPED past Tim and Paul, shrilling like a madman, and the boys themselves whooped and screeched in frantic glee. They charged through the creek like a squadron of cavalry, sweeping the Comanche ponies in front of them. The horses kicked up great fountains of water and lunged up the far bank in a jostling mob, whinnying as if to echo the cheers of the men.

Next they were racing across the empty prairie, and left the village behind. The ponies' hoofs made a muffled drumming on the dry earth, the sound half drowning the hideous outcries and yells from the camp. Gradually the cries faded with distance, until they could be heard no longer.

They travelled fast for a good many miles before halting to blow the horses. By now the stars had paled, and faint streaks of grey marked the sky, low down in the east. The horses were visible as separate animals instead of as a vague mass; their ribs heaved and the dawn breeze whipped their manes as they clustered timidly together.

Once more they listened. Tim did not believe

he would ever lose the habit, after this. Always you listened, straining your ears to catch the slightest rustle or scrape which might be a Comanche near you. Because, if you didn't, you were their meat.

Pechuga sat bareback on his pony, looking back with his head cocked on one side under its huge tall-crowned *sombrero*. The *sombrero* had once been ornamented with silver braid, very showy, but now most of the braid had worn off and the remainder was tarnished.

Brazos watched him and, after a space, queried, "Hear anything?"

The Mexican shook his head. "Hear nothing yet," he replied. "Mebbe later on." He seemed worried.

"They won't catch us," grinned Brazos. His white teeth flashed as he looked at Tim. "That was quite a party," he said. "I sure didn't figure we'd work it as easy as that."

Oddly, Tim could not help smiling back at him. It did not matter that both these men were outlaws and villains; this was the second time they had helped Paul and himself out of a bad spot. Besides, there was a quality in them which he could not resist. A kind of reckless enjoyment of life, which they refused to take seriously. But, in spite of that, his common sense made him realise that they were still scoundrels who would bear plenty of watching.

"It was too lively for my liking," he answered Brazos. "Me, I enjoy parties better without arrows!"

"All the same it was fun," declared Paul. His hat was crammed down over his ears, and the tuft of hair stuck out of the torn crown like a cock's feathers. "Don't remember that I ever enjoyed a ride as much as that!"

"You ain't done ridin' yet, kid," Brazos told him. "We'll have to git through a heap more butt-polishin', before we git clear of those red babes, believe yuh me!" He got down and twisted his rope into a rough bridle, Indian style, around his mount's lower jaw.

The others followed his example. Looking at the other horses, Tim asked, "What do you aim to do with the ponies?"

"Do with 'em?" asked Brazos in surprise. "Why, hang on to 'em, of course! They're worth money."

"But . . . !" Tim was going to object that it was stealing, only he checked himself because it sounded foolish. He saw the two outlaws laughing at him, and felt himself go scarlet as he guessed they knew what was in his mind.

"Ain't it too bad?" mocked Brazos. "I forgot yuh ain't partial to hoss-thieves!"

"Mebbe we should take the ponies back again?" suggested Pechuga. He looked so comical, with his shoe-button eyes twinkling and his face pulled into a sad, repentant grimace, that the boys had to laugh at him.

"But they'll slow us down, won't they?" said Paul. "We'd split the breeze a heap faster, if we didn't have to drive them."

"That's so," Brazos agreed, "but the Injuns are travellin' slower still. They're walkin', remember? And Comanches like walkin' just about as much as a fellow with earache enjoys a brass band concert. They won't catch up on us."

But Pechuga was less confident. "Is true what the boy says," he objected. "Say they have other broncs some place, tied up outside their lodges? They come after us pretty queeck then, I guess!"

Brazos pulled his thin moustache and pondered. "Yuh could be right, at that," he admitted after a pause. Then he grinned again, and added, "Mustn't miss out on any chances. From here on we'll watch our back trail real close. Now let's drift!"

They set off, hazing the ponies along, moving north-eastward at a smart lope. It was broad daylight when they halted again. They drove the horses into a dry gulley, carved from the ground by a flood at some former time, and dismounted. The gulley, or wash, hid them from sight. Nobody could find them there except by accident.

Naturally they did not light a fire. There was no point in that, anyhow, as they had nothing to cook. For their meal they took a Mexican breakfast; that is, took their belts in a notch, and rested for a while.

The wash looked out on a broad shallow valley. From where he sprawled, Tim could see a long way; a horizon-wide stretch of burnt brown grass, rolling to meet the rich blue sky. It was quite empty. In it there was nothing that moved, except the eternally rippling grass.

All morning they had kept a sharp watch behind them, but had seen no hint of pursuit. In itself, that meant nothing, because Comanches would not have let themselves be seen; but they were fairly sure that the Indians had no horses to chase them with.

"Gee, I could eat," said Paul wistfully. "Haven't had a bite, since they gave us those charred moccasins on sticks, yesterday."

"Sorry. Yuh'll have to go hungry for a while," Brazos told him, "unless yuh try a chaw of grass or somethin'. Horses make out pretty good on it."

Paul replied that it might be so but, as he wasn't a bronc, nor any kin to the late King Nebuchadnezzar so far as he knew, he guessed he'd let the whole thing go. Tim was hungry, too. He put the thought of food out of his mind; there was no sense in fretting about it, if none was to be had.

Instead, he remembered his manners, a little late. "Thanks for getting us out of there," he said to the two men. "We're a heap obliged."

"Think nothin' of it," said Brazos. "We was goin' out of there anyhow, an' reckoned yuh might feel like comin' along with us."

"How did you get away?" asked Paul eagerly.

"Why, we jest said good-bye, an' drifted. There wasn't anythin' to it, only the fond farewells."

"They must have been touching," Tim snickered. "That old Coup-Counter was right set on you staying, from what I could make out."

Pechuga snickered too. Pechuga had a flat broad face and, when he laughed, his small black-currant eyes almost vanished in the creases of his lids. "Coup-Counter have some bad luck," he explained. "A leetle accident. He excused us."

Tim's laugh ended abruptly. Shocked, he wished he hadn't asked the question. Too well he knew the reputation of this pair; both were gunmen and killers. He could not put his thoughts into words, but once again Brazos sensed what was in his mind.

"Yuh're wrong," said the outlaw mockingly. "I jest leaned the barrel of my six-gun against his coconut, and he kind of lost interest in the proceedings. I guess that was one coup that counted against him."

"He'll make things tough for you, if he finds you again," said Tim uneasily. "Maybe we'd better get going."

"I expect he'll be madder than a wild hog with

shingles," Brazos admitted. "but there's no hurry for a minute or two. He ain't goin' to catch up with us."

"Where are we heading?" asked Tim.

Brazos turned and looked at him then. Instantly Tim knew that the leopard had not changed his spots after all. Once again he caught the full impact of the outlaw's dark magnetic stare, full of baleful recklessness. Brazos grinned; the wide white dog's grin, which was a sure sign he was planning devilment.

"Well," drawled Brazos, "I ain't absolutely sure, yet. I ain't had time to lay many plans." When the boys said nothing, he went on, "Yuh see, it's this way. Yuh know I was after your Dad's trail-herd. I was fixin' to jump your outfit a bit later on, when they were about near the Kansas line, but things kind of got snarled up. But now I have a better idea!"

"What d'you mean?" Tim's throat was dry.

"Why, I figure I'm entitled to some compensation, for kidnappin' yuh two from ol' Coup-Counter. I aim to let your Dad know I've got yuh both. Then he can drive the herd to Dodge an' sell it, an' meet me with the money he gits for it afterwards. Seems to me that ought to save ever'body a heap of trouble."

"Why, you two-timing old varmint!" Paul burst out. "You'd do that, after—after. . . !" Paul stopped, unable to control his feelings.

"Go easy on the hard words," protested Brazos reproachfully. "I dunno how yuh can say I'm two-timin' yuh, for I never promised either of yuh a thing, only that me an' Pechuga would try to git yuh clear of them savages."

"I was beginning to think you weren't as bad as folks made out," Tim's voice was quiet, but very bitter. "I guess I was wrong, that's all. You got us out of two bad spots, but it doesn't look like we'll have much to thank you for in the end."

"Sorry, kid. Business is business." Brazos looked slightly uncomfortable. "I have to make an honest dime wherever I can."

Silence followed. Sourly Tim gazed out at the prairie again. Still it held no sign of life until, far off, a flock of grouse rocketed out of the grass and flew away to settle in another spot. By instinct, his eyes searched the area, although he was not thinking what he was doing. The birds came from a spot near the crest of a long slope and, as Tim stared, a bright sparkle flashed fleetingly on the very top of the slope against the vivid sky.

He was about to look away, when the meaning of it hit him so hard that he was petrified for an instant. Then he was on his feet, grabbing for his pony. Brazos was on him at once. The outlaw moved with the speed of a lunging snake, caught him by the arm as he reached Biscuit.

"No, yuh don't!" said Brazos. "Cool off, kid. It won't do yuh no good to try an' run."

"It won't?" Tim flung back, and laughed shrilly. "It won't do any of us any good to stay around here, either. Look over there!"

Still holding him tight, Brazos whirled to stare back across the prairie, as Pechuga and Paul jumped up. "¡Ay, *mi alma!*" breathed Pechuga. "They come!"

Over the crest of the slope rode a bunch of mounted Indians.

CHAPTER EIGHTEEN

CANADIAN RIVER

BRAZOS LET GO of Tim and jumped for his pony. "Let's dust!" he said briefly. In a flash they were all mounted. Brazos ran the captured ponies out of the wash, and sent them at a dead run in front of him.

"You taking them along, still?" Tim said, angrily.

"Sure, why not? They may come in handy yet." Brazos threw a look back, and added, "No use to play it careful. They saw us before we moved."

They were only just in time. The Comanches were coming fast, in a ragged, screeching wave. The Indians goaded their broncs to top speed, and tore down the long grassy slope in pursuit. They were about half a mile away.

In the lead, Tim was sure he recognised Coup-Counter, and next to the chief was the man with the horse-brasses in his hair, the buck who had stolen Biscuit. It was the glint of the sun on the brass ornaments which Tim had seen, when the Indian peered over the top of the slope to spy on them.

The fugitives sat down to ride. Guns banged

behind them, mingling with the shrill yelps of the Comanches. Tim bent low over Biscuit's withers. This was the first time he had ever been shot at, and he didn't like it.

"Don't worry about the guns, boys," Brazos said, with a hint of contempt. "They couldn't hit a Conestoga wagon at ten yards any time, an' now they're some excited." He was riding straight up, sparing a glance backward now and again, and even waved in ribald insult.

"It's the arrows yuh have to watch out for," he went on. "They're real good with them, when they git in range."

After a while, Tim glimpsed the Indians when he looked back over his shoulder. There were only nine of them; not a hundred, which they had seemed like to him at first.

Probably that number was all they could find mounts for. No doubt Pechuga had been right, when he suggested that the Comanches had a few ponies staked out apart from the main herd. Tim thought the Indians were gaining on them. Surely they were nearer than when they made their rush down the slope?

Brazos lost his grin, and was giving all his mind to making progress. The Mexican too looked serious, his small black eyes continually darting glances behind him. After a while Brazos said, "They're goin' to catch up on us pretty soon. Then we'll have to fight."

A fat chance they were going to have, too, thought Tim. Four of them, only two of whom had pistols, against nine heavily-armed braves!

"Cheer up," called Brazos, breaking into his thoughts. "See that ahead?"

A long line of timber straggled a mile or so ahead of them, wandering in curves across the prairie. Tim nodded. "A creek," he answered. "What of it?"

"That's the Canadian River," said Brazos. "We'll lose 'em there."

Tim hoped that was true, but didn't share the outlaw's certainty. Even in his short experience of them, he knew that Comanches took a heap of losing. He didn't think the brush would help much either, not when he remembered the sneaky way they got around.

But Brazos was talking again. "It's tough," Brazos shook his head sadly. "It sure is hard! Every time me an' Pechuga try to round up a few dollars lately, somethin' cuts us out of our profit!"

"What d'ye mean?" asked Paul, thinking that Brazos meant to let the captured horses go at last.

"I aim to git shed of yuh kids," Brazos replied. "It ain't good business, to let yuh ride clear back to your outfit, but I'll jest have to cut my losses on that deal. Now here's what I want yuh to do. . . !"

Quickly he explained what was in his mind.

After they pushed their broncs hard, they had to make the river before the Comanches gained too much ground on them. They had to.

The line of trees grew nearer, and they sent the horses racing frantically in a wild dash for shelter. The Indians had closed the gap to within a few hundred yards, and were no more than a long arrow-shot behind. Already a number of shafts were dropping at their heels with an ugly reach of power and accuracy.

Then they were in the brush. "Now!" cried Brazos. He smiled at them briefly, his drawn six-shooter in his hand, and added, "Good luck!" Pechuga too waved and smiled, without speaking. He too had a pistol, and his long knife was bared.

The boys drove straight on down the bank at the river, leaving the outlaws and the stolen horses behind. Branches whipped at their faces and jagged their clothes, but they slammed through and hit the water at full tilt. The river was not high, but was fairly wide. It took them several minutes to cross. Luckily they did not have to swim far.

Guns crashed behind them as they heeled their mounts up the north bank into the shelter of the timber. Hidden in the cottonwoods which grew thick along the river's edge, they paused to listen and let the ponies get back their wind.

Pandemonium broke out on the bank they had left. Guns exploded in a scattered angry fusillade, mingled with yells and screeches. The reports of the guns were uneven in tone, the dull bangs of the Comanche smoothbores heavier than the lighter crash of revolvers. War-whoops lifted, high-pitched and quavering, above the din.

For a space the boys lingered, absorbed in the fight and lost to all else. They could see little of what went on, because of the trees, and had to guess what was happening.

Then Tim came to himself and realised what they had to do. "Come on," he jerked out abruptly. "We'd better get going."

"Can't we stay a while, and watch?" Paul objected. "I ain't seen anything yet, hardly."

"Not on your life. Brazos said for us to keep moving down river, and that's what we're going to do!"

"All right, but it's a pity," Paul grumbled. "I'd like to see a real fight. She sure sounds like a humdinger, don't she?"

Tim nodded, turning Biscuit. "Sure does," he agreed. "Maybe we can send help, if we run across the outfit soon."

"Not much chance, is there? We've been gone from there more than two days."

Gloomily, Tim realised that was true. As matters stood, Brazos and Pechuga were way out on a limb; and, as Paul said, there was not much hope of finding their own outfit in time to be of help. It came to him then that Brazos and the

Mexican must have known that quite well, when they told him and Paul to keep going. The outlaws had stopped to hold off the Comanches, so that the boys would have a chance of escape.

Why had they done that, he wondered? He did not know what to make of Brazos, or Pechuga either, for that matter. Sometimes they seemed good, decent fellows and then, before you knew it, they were planning some bad thing or other, and seemed to find it a joke.

One thing was certain. Neither of them, bad men and owlhooters though they might be, was nearly as bad as the reputation they carried. He tried to decide how many upright, law-abiding citizens would have taken on odds of nine to two, simply in order to let two youngsters make a break.

He and Paul rode downstream, keeping well in the shelter of the brush. The fight still went on behind them, amid the trees on the other bank. Now and then they paused to look back, but there was not much to be seen. The shots were spaced farther apart now, and the yelling had died down, but a whoop now and again lifted in a blood-freezing howl.

After a time the sounds grew faint with distance, and they relaxed their pace. Going to the edge of the bank, they peered upstream for several minutes. During their ride, the river had made a number of winding turns, and they had to look across country at the spot where they had forded it.

"I don't hear anything," said Paul. "Must be all over by now." He spoke tightly, as if there was something in his throat.

Tim felt much the same as Paul did, sad and proud and miserable. He wished he knew what had happened back there, but was afraid it could have ended only in one way. In spite of that, he said, "Maybe they got clear. They were real tough *hombres*; even Coup-Counter and his braves would find them a tough mouthful to chaw on."

"Maybe," Paul nodded doubtfully. "Sure hope they did. Those Comanches must have busted a few teeth while they were chawing, whichever way it went. Say, look!" he broke off excitedly, "Somebody's splitting the breeze over there!"

A dust-cloud lifted slowly above the drab green of the brush, to hang in the sky. It was too big to have been made by any but a large bunch of horses. The boys stared at it, trying to convince themselves that Brazos and Pechuga were driving the pony herd, but believed in their hearts that the Comanches had got the horses back again.

The sun glittered on the bright water, flowing past them, and the breeze ruffled the tops of the trees. There was no sound to be heard from upstream. Head hanging, Tim mounted Biscuit again and turned the pony with his knees and the rawhide hackamore he had rigged from the Comanche *reata*. "Let's go," he said shortly. "Nothing to loaf around for, any longer."

Neither spoke for a long time after that. As Brazos had told them to do, they kept a sharp lookout all around them, because there was no telling whether the Indians were still after them. Their escape was a wound to Coup-Counter's pride, and it was likely that the Indian would try hard to catch them, to square the matter off.

Late in the afternoon Tim said, "Don't think they'll git us, if we have luck. It'll be dark soon, and to-morrow we might pick up the outfit."

"You figure Brazos was right, saying that the outfit would have crossed the Canadian by now. if it had kept going?" said Paul.

"He said 'if'," Tim pointed out. "If they haven't, they must still be somewhere around the place where we left them. We'll scout around the bank for tracks, to-morrow. If we don't find any, we'll hit south again."

"Did you mean that, about those savages not getting us?" queried Paul, later.

Tim was not as sure as he had sounded, but he never believed in looking at the blue side of things. "Sure," he said stoutly. "Why not?"

Paul pointed across the river. His hand trembled slightly. "More riders over there," he said.

CHAPTER NINETEEN

The Long Return

Sure enough, a faint film of dust smoked above the trees on the far bank. As they watched it, drifted and settled. They checked their mounts and waited, their hearts in their mouths, trying to tell themselves that it was only a trick of the wind, or that it had not really been there. That it was anything, except the awful reality.

"Think they've seen us?" whispered Paul.

Tim gulped. "No," his voice was tight and choked. "I guess not. If they had, we wouldn't have seen any dust, you can bet . . . We wouldn't have seen anything at all, until they jumped us!"

He remembered the way the Comanches had crept up on them the other time. Only an accidental flash of sunlight on a warrior's headdress had warned them; it was too much to hope for such luck twice running. He looked at Paul. "Looks like they got . . . !" he began, but stopped. He could not go on.

Paul nodded dumbly. Both boys were badly scared, never doubting for a moment that the Comanches had caught up with them again. They did not know what to do. Then, strained to breaking-point, Paul's nerve stampeded him into action. "Let's ride for it!" he said, and kicked his bronc into a flying run.

Instinctively Tim let Biscuit go too, and they raced blindly through the willows and cotton-woods. Clinging to the backs of their ponies, they lay flat and let the branches scrape over them. They knew plenty about brush-riding; had done it ever since they could remember, back home.

Yells lifted across the river. Tim knew then that they had done the wrong thing. If they had lain low, the riders might have passed without finding them, but it was too late now. Their only chance was to keep fogging it, and trust to keeping ahead until nightfall. In the dark they might have a better chance to get clear.

It drifted through his alarm that the yelling was not of the kind that Indians mostly used, and he took a glance over his shoulder uncertainly. Horsemen were crossing the river, a bunch of them set off by the slimming sheen of the water. Unbelievingly, Tim hauled up to watch them.

He sat there like a statue for a full minute. Then he gave a screech that would have scared Coup-Counter himself. Snatching off his hat, he waved it crazily and turned Biscuit to go barrel-ling back to meet the riders.

In a few strides he was sure. Already he had recognised the other party as white men; now, seeing the old buckskin jacket worn by the leader, he was in transports of joy and relief. He came to a skidding halt on the bank, just as they came wading up through the shallows.

"Dad!" he yelled. "Dad, is it really you?"

Paul came back in the middle of the greetings. His brothers Ollie and Layton were so pleased to see him that they hauled him from the pony and manhandled him with delighted rudeness, until he yelled for mercy.

"How did you get away from the Indians?" asked Cal Bryant, when feelings had simmered down enough for them to talk. His lean, bronzed features were alight with gratitude, and the lightening of the worry that had been grinding into his soul.

The boys explained hurriedly, blurting out their tale in a jumble of mixed-up snatches. "We left Brazos and Pechuga up the river, standing the Comanches off," Tim finished, his pleasure dying when he thought of that. "I—I guess Coup-Counter's bunch must have rubbed them out."

"How far back?" asked his father.

"Two-three hours' ride. We saw a big dust cloud after we left. It looked like the Comanches had taken their broncs back; the cloud was too big to be made by a small bunch of horses."

Mr. Bryant nodded. "We owe it to those fellows to go and see what happened," he said. "After what they did for you boys, I'd be glad to give 'em the herd, if it belonged to me. Let's go!"

They remained on the north bank of the Canadian, travelling in the shelter of the timber and taking care to lift no more dust than they could help. It was late twilight when they reached the spot where Brazos and the Mexican had made their stand.

All was silent there. After they halted and listened, Cal Bryant said, "Stay here, and keep quiet. I'm going across to see what I can find. Doesn't look like there's anybody over there now."

They waited whilst he rode out into the open and walked his pony down into the river. Tim watched, his mouth dry with suspense, but no shot came from the dusk-laden cottonwoods on the other side. Cal Bryant rode into the brush, and vanished.

After a while, when it was almost dark, he came out again, and forded the stream back to where they waited for him. "All gone," he said briefly. "Two dead broncs, but that's all."

"You mean they got clear?" Tim asked eagerly. His father looked at him sombrely. "I hope they did," he said. "Because, if they didn't, they're past anybody's help now. The Comanches would take them back to the village." He said no more, but the boys knew what he meant. It would be better to die fighting, than have to face that.

"Any use trying to go for the village?" asked Will Dunford. "Do the boys know where it is?"

"No use at all," Mr. Bryant replied. "In the first place, we couldn't get there in time to do any good. And in the second, we'd only be more guys for a Comanche party, if we got there. Six of us, including two unarmed boys, would be easy meat for them. I don't know if you ever heard about it, but Comanches are real bad medicine to tangle with."

"We go back, then?" Layton Barr sounded disappointed.

"We go back," Cal Bryant repeated. "We still have a herd to take up to Dodge, remember?"

"What happened to the herd?" Paul asked.

"We left it grazing, and came out here to see if we could find you boys, but we lost the sign. Those Comanche friends of yours hid their tracks pretty neatly."

"You mean the beef is back yonder, with nobody to look after it?"

"Frenchy Debrelle's there, and Lester. They can't do much, except try to stop 'em wandering too far," said Ollie Barr. "Likely we'll have to spend a week rounding the critters up, when we hit camp again."

"Let's hope not," said Cal Bryant. "Anyhow it has its good side. We have the boys back, and while we're gone, the steers will be putting on meat. They'll be all the better for that, when we hit market."

"How did you get here, anyhow?" asked Will

Dunford. "I guess you had to run whichever way you could, uh?"

Tim inclined his head. "Brazos brought us here, and told us to hit down river," he explained. "He said we'd likely find your tracks, if you'd crossed with the herd. If you hadn't, we'd know you were still south of the Canadian, and would have to look for you, so he said."

"He seems to have been something better than the renegade we thought he was," admitted Cal Bryant. "All the same, I'd like to have seen the brands on those cows he says he bought from the Indians. I never heard of any Indian owning cattle, unless he'd stolen them."

He glanced around, then dismounted. "We'll camp here for to-night," he said. "It'll be safe, I guess. The Indians aren't likely to come back here, but we won't light a fire, in case."

"Did you bring anything to eat?" asked Paul.

"Some jerky," said Will Dunford. "I guess it's a mite tough for young stomachs, though. Besides, I seem to remember that yuh don't go big licks on it."

"I'd try to make out on some, if I had it," said Paul. "Give me about a hundredweight and a half, and I'll see if I like it any better than I did."

Jerky was not so bad, when you hadn't eaten anything for more than thirty hours.

It took them two more days to get back to the

outfit. As Cal Bryant had said, the steers were widely scattered. Tim saw them, grazing in twos and threes over a broad stretch of prairie, before they came within hailing distance. There was one lone rider who made a wide circle around the herd and turned back those who were farthest out.

The rider was the cowhand Lester, who took off his hat and whooped when he saw them. He was a stranger to them before the drive began, but they regarded him now as an old and trusted friend, although they had not known him for more than a few weeks.

He came tearing towards them, grinning and scattering the steers. "If he starts them running," growled Cal Bryant, "I'll take the time off his pay, when we get to Kansas."

But the cows did not run. "So yuh got back!" Lester cried. "Bully for yuh! We was all figuring you'd be wearin' warpaint an' feathers by now. How are yuh feelin'?"

"Hungry," said Paul. "Where's the chuck-wagon? I aim to strike Frenchy for a meal, soon as I get close enough to talk to him."

"My, my!" drawled Will. "I never saw anybody with such a one-track mind. I figure that tale of yours about escapin' from the Comanches is all a lot of baloney. The truth is that they ran yuh out of camp before yuh ate 'em clear down to the bone."

"If you'd ever tried Comanche grub, you

wouldn't say that," Paul countered darkly. "They scorch old bootsoles around the edges and serve 'em up on sticks. Makes jerky taste like fried chicken, believe yuh us!"

They reached the chuck-wagon and dismounted. Frenchy was stumping around, and did not see them at once. When he did, he hugged them like a bear, chortling through his whiskers and crowing.

"Yuh young scalawags!" he cried. "Where in tarnation did yuh spring from?"

"Glad to see us, Frenchy?" Tim was quite touched by the cook's welcome. It was so different from the way he remembered him; in the old days, Frenchy would rather have died than admitted that he liked anything or anybody.

"Of course I'm glad," bellowed Frenchy. He loosed them, and his expression changed. "Yuh think I *like* doin' all the doggone camp chores?" he demanded. "No? Well, then, if yuh aim to eat to-night, yuh can begin on peelin' that sack of spuds right now, the pair of yuh!"

Frenchy hadn't changed so much after all, they thought, as they began on the potatoes.

CHAPTER TWENTY

A LATE SURPRISE

DODGE IS some town!" Tim told his mother. He could not find words to describe it properly, so she would understand. "You never saw so many folks in all your life. And the stores—they're grand, full of all kind of stuff. Guns and saddles, and silver bridles. They even have ploughs, in some of 'em."

Mrs. Bryant smiled, listening to him. She did not care two hoots about Dodge, so long as her boy had come back safe. She spared a thought for Ramon Chavez and his wife, grieving over poor Vicente, and felt for them. It might as easily have been Tim.

Tim went on talking. He did not say much about the Indians, only that Brazos and Pechuga had rescued Paul and himself. Louise was playing with the doll he had brought her, putting the doll to bed in an old butter-box. The doll had red-painted cheeks and a blue dress, and had been named " Mamie", and Louise kept yelling, " Mamie go by-byes!" whilst he talked.

The herd had reached Dodge three weeks after the escape from the Comanches, without any further incident. On the way up, Cal Bryant sent Lester to Fort Supply with a message about the Indian incident, and a troop of cavalry went to look for Coup-Counter.

Later, the Bryant outfit heard that the soldiers did not find him. They found no trace of Brazos or Pechuga either. The third member of the trio, Rusty, had been killed by the Comanches soon after he left Coup-Counter's village, when Tim and Paul were taken there. Some evidence was found that proved this, although no charges were ever brought against anyone.

After selling the herd, the outfit spent a few days in Dodge, sight-seeing and having a good time. Then they rode home. The trip home was a heap faster than the journey north, not being delayed by the slow-moving cattle, and they reached McMullen County in less than a month after they started back.

Since then there had been a round of visits to friends. With the money from the herd, now divided between its owners, prospects were brighter in the neighbourhood. It was already decided that another herd was to go north, as soon as was practicable; probably early next year, everybody said. And Cal Bryant was to be trail boss again.

Paul and Tim were no longer treated as children. You couldn't behave that way to seasoned trail hands; they were men! Only Mrs. Barr gave Tim a lecture when she heard that Paul had been laying around in the damp. "I told you not to let him do that," she scolded, "And the minute my back's turned, you set around and watch him catch his death. A fine friend you are, to be sure! You know he's delicate!"

Tim knew that Paul was about as delicate as a longhorn bull, fed high on mesquite beans and spring grass, but did not argue. Mrs. Barr seemed to think getting wet was worse than being captured by Indians, and that Tim could have prevented either, if he had taken the trouble. However, she relented when she had said her piece, and gave them a cake she had baked especially for them. They sat outside and ate it, sitting on the corral rail and looking at the old sorrel pony Paul used to ride. Tonto, now older and beginning to get a glimmer of sense, came in for a share of the cake crumbs.

"Say, do you figure those two fellows ever got clear of Coup-Counter?" said Paul, in a muffled voice. Cake hampers clear speech at times.

"No savvy," Tim answered. He had wondered about it himself, often. "Hope they did. Maybe Coup-Counter didn't git away from them, either. You know Indians always take away their dead, if they can."

Paul grunted. "They were outlaws," he said, "but for me they rate good an' high. I hope nobody ever catches them."

Nothing was ever heard of Brazos or Pechuga again. But, many years later, when Tim was a grown man and an experienced trail boss himself, he drove a herd one time from Goliad in Texas to a place near Maricopas, in Arizona Territory. The cattle were to be delivered to a Mr. W. Smith, a well-known rancher in that part of the world.

It was a bad trip, more than a thousand miles, of which a big slice was across almost waterless desert, but Tim made it without too many losses from thirst and trail-weariness. Luckily he met no Apaches, who were then on the warpath against the whites.

The herd was of breeder cows, to stock the new ranges of Arizona, and he nursed them along as best he could, resting them for a while in the valley of the Rio Grande del Norte until they picked up again in strength. Then he took them on to their new owner.

Mr. Smith met the herd a few miles west of his ranch. He was a lean, whipcord-tough individual with iron-grey hair and a neatly trimmed grey beard. He had his Mexican foreman with him.

"Pleased to meet yuh, Mr. Bryant," he said, putting out a hand. "Yuh brought 'em through in fine shape. Still, I guess that's to be expected from a man with your experience on cattle-trails!"

"Thanks for the compliment," said Tim. It was dusk, and he could not see the rancher's face distinctly. The foreman was riding around the herd, sizing up the cattle, but something about the way he sat in his saddle was familiar.

"We lost thirty on the trail," he said. "Mostly from drinking bad water. It's tough trying to keep them from these poison alkali wells when they're thirsty."

"Sure, I understand," said Smith. He was looking at Tim curiously in the twilight. "Trailing beef is no tenderfoot's game. Less than two per cent. loss on a drive like yuh had to make is nothin' to grumble about."

The Mexican foreman rode towards them then. Smith waved him back, with a motion that he did not want Tim to see, but Tim did not miss it. "All right," Tim said. "Let him come. I have an awful bad memory for some things."

Smith grinned then. Beneath his grey beard his teeth showed very white; the grin was rather like that of a dog; a wise, good-tempered dog, but not one to be fooled around with. The foreman grinned, too. He had small eyes like currants in a bun, which vanished into creases in his face.

"How!" said the foreman, putting out a hand. "Sure glad to see yuh, *señor*! You very welcome."

"I'm with that sentiment," said Mr. Smith. "Stay with us, and visit a while, uh?"

"Thanks," said Tim. "I'm obliged for the invitation. Maybe I will."

It was some days before the talk got around to

the adventures of two notorious owlhooters and cattle-thieves called Brazos and Pechuga. The subject came up casually in the conversation, which had begun with old times in Texas. Both Mr. Smith and his foreman Luis were Texans, it seemed.

"I remember them," said the rancher. "Real bad boys they were. But Comanches got 'em, so I heard."

"I often wondered," said Tim. "They say the devil looks after his own. Paul and I used to hope they'd made it, because they were both ace-high with us."

"They might have had their good points. But, of course, we're mighty respectable around here. Don't have any truck with folks like that. No, sir!" Smith shook his head, and grinned his doggy grin.

"Ever'bodee know we're honest," said Luis modestly. "Been around here for long time. No steal, no rob anybodee. Good people, us!"

Tim nodded, keeping his face straight. "I think they might have dodged the Comanches," he said. "But I can't figure out how they did it. It would be interesting to know."

"Guess it would," Smith agreed. "Only they didn't, did they?"

"So you say. I have my own notion about it; though, of course I wouldn't argue. It would be silly, in the face of the evidence."

"Some things are too silly to have an explanation," drawled Smith. His dark eyes contrasted with his iron grey hair and whiskers. They were hard and brilliant, alight with reckless amusement as he spoke.

"Say two fellows were chased by Indians, and had a bunch of ponies along that they'd lifted from the Indian village," he went on. "They might have stood the Comanches off for a while, and then loosed the ponies. If the bucks wanted the ponies bad enough—more than the whites' scalps, that is—they might take out after the horses."

"Would they do that?" Tim asked.

Smith nodded. "They would, if the ponies were all that their band owned. If they didn't, the whole band would be afoot; and that's worse than being dead, to a Comanche. Then the two fellows might sneak off in the brush, and git clear. As I say, it's unlikely, but it might have happened."

"But it didn't happen?" said Tim.

"No," said Mr. Smith firmly. "Brazos and Pechuga are dead and buried. Me, I aim to let them stay that way. I'm a respectable rancher, in case you don't know it!"